E. Hemingway 著

吳勞 譯

THE OLD MAN AND THE SEA

老人與海

商務印書館

本書譯文由上海世紀出版股份有限公司譯文出版社授權使用

Photo Credits: Shutterstock; Freshwater and Marine Image Bank

書　　名：*The Old Man and the Sea* 老人與海

作　　者：E. Hemingway

譯　　者：吳　勞

責任編輯：仇茵晴

封面設計：楊愛文

出　　版：商務印書館 (香港) 有限公司

　　　　　香港筲箕灣耀興道 3 號東滙廣場 8 樓

　　　　　http://www.commercialpress.com.hk

發　　行：香港聯合書刊物流有限公司

　　　　　香港新界大埔汀麗路 36 號中華商務印刷大廈 3 字樓

印　　刷：中華商務彩色印刷有限公司

　　　　　香港新界大埔汀麗路 36 號中華商務印刷大廈

版　　次：2018 年 3 月第 1 版第 2 次印刷

　　　　　© 2016 商務印書館 (香港) 有限公司

　　　　　ISBN 978 962 07 0444 4

　　　　　Printed in Hong Kong

Publisher's Note 出版説明

　　老人説過:"能走運當然更好,不過我情願把所有的事情都做到分毫不差。等運氣來臨時,就有所準備了。"老人也説過:"人可以被毀滅,但不能被打敗。"老人用行動實踐着他的諾言。是甚麼使老人有着如此堅定的信念?這是值得我們讀者思考的問題。

　　初、中級英語程度讀者使用本書時,先閱讀英文原文,如遇到理解障礙,則參考中譯作為輔助。在英文原文結束之前或附註解,標註古英語、非現代詞彙拼寫形式及語法;同樣,在譯文結束之前或會附註釋,以幫助讀者理解原文故事背景。如有餘力,讀者可在閱讀原文部份段落後,查閱相應中譯,觀察同樣詞句在雙語中不同的表達。

　　在經歷了重重困難和磨難後,老人還是積極地準備着下次出海的工具。在現實生活中,我們能否也保持這份堅韌與執着,勇敢地面對生活?

商務印書館 (香港) 有限公司
編輯出版部

Contents　目錄

To Charles Scribner
And
To Max Perkins

He was an old man who fished alone in a skiff in the Gulf Stream and he had gone eighty-four days now without taking a fish. In the first forty days a boy had been with him. But after forty days without a fish the boy's parents had told him that the old man was now definitely and finally *salao*, which is the worst form of unlucky, and the boy had gone at their orders in another boat which caught three good fish the first week. It made the boy sad to see the old man come in each day with his skiff empty and he always went down to help him carry either the coiled lines or the gaff and harpoon and the sail that was furled around the mast. The sail was patched with flour sacks and, furled, it looked like the flag of permanent defeat.

The old man was thin and gaunt with deep wrinkles in the back of his neck. The brown blotches of the benevolent skin cancer the sun brings from its reflection on the tropic sea were on his cheeks. The blotches ran well down the sides of his face and his hands had the deep-creased scars from handling heavy fish on the cords. But none of these scars were fresh. They were as old as erosions in a fishless desert.

Everything about him was old except his eyes and they were the same colour as the sea and were cheerful and undefeated.

'Santiago,' the boy said to him as they climbed the bank from where the skiff was hauled up. 'I could go with you again. We've made some money.'

The old man had taught the boy to fish and the boy loved him.

'No,' the old man said. 'You're with a lucky boat. Stay with them.'

'But remember how you went eighty-seven days without fish and then we caught big ones every day for three weeks.'

'I remember,' the old man said. 'I know you did not leave me because you doubted.'

'It was papa made me leave. I am a boy and I must obey him.'

'I know,' the old man said. 'It is quite normal.'

'He hasn't much faith.'

'No,' the old man said. 'But we have. Haven't we?'

'Yes,' the boy said. 'Can I offer you a beer on the Terrace and then we'll take the stuff home.'

'Why not?' the old man said. 'Between fishermen.'

They sat on the Terrace and many of the fishermen made fun of the old man and he was not angry. Others, of the older fishermen, looked at him and were sad. But they did not show it and they spoke politely about the current and the depths they had drifted their lines at and the steady good weather and of what they had seen. The successful fishermen of that day were already in and had butchered their marlin out and carried them laid full length across two planks, with two men staggering at the end of each plank, to the fish house where they waited for the ice truck to carry them to the market in Havana. Those who had caught sharks had taken them to the shark factory on the other side of the cove where they were hoisted on a block and tackle, their livers removed, their fins cut off and their hides skinned out and their flesh cut into strips for salting.

When the wind was in the east a smell came across the harbour from the shark factory; but today there was only the faint edge of the odor because the wind had backed into the north and then dropped off and it was pleasant and sunny on the Terrace.

'Santiago,' the boy said.

'Yes,' the old man said. He was holding his glass and thinking of many years ago.

'Can I go out to get sardines for you for tomorrow?'

'No. Go and play baseball. I can still row and Rogelio will throw the net.'

'I would like to go. If I cannot fish with you, I would like to serve in some way.'

'You bought me a beer,' the old man said. 'You are already a man.'

'How old was I when you first took me in a boat?'

'Five and you nearly were killed when I brought the fish in too green and he nearly tore the boat to pieces. Can you remember?'

'I can remember the tail slapping and banging and the thwart breaking and the noise of the clubbing. I can remember you throwing me into the bow where the wet coiled lines were and feeling the whole boat shiver and the noise of you clubbing him like chopping a tree down and the sweet blood smell all over me.'

'Can you really remember that or did I just tell it to you?'

'I remember everything from when we first went together.'

The old man looked at him with his sunburned, confident loving eyes.

'If you were my boy I'd take you out and gamble,' he said. 'But you are your father's and your mother's and you are in a lucky boat.'

'May I get the sardines? I know where I can get four baits too.'

'I have mine left from today. I put them in salt in the box.'

'Let me get four fresh ones.'

'One,' the old man said. His hope and his confidence had never gone. But now they were freshening as when the breeze rises.

'Two,' the boy said.

'Two,' the old man agreed. 'You didn't steal them?'

'I would,' the boy said. 'But I bought these.'

'Thank you,' the old man said. He was too simple to wonder when he had attained humility. But he knew he had attained it and he knew it was not disgraceful and it carried no loss of true pride.

'Tomorrow is going to be a good day with this current,' he said.

'Where are you going?' the boy asked.

'Far out to come in when the wind shifts. I want to be out before it is light.'

'I'll try to get him to work far out,' the boy said. 'Then if you hook something truly big we can come to your aid.'

'He does not like to work too far out.'

'No,' the boy said. 'But I will see something that he cannot see such as a bird working and get him to come out after dolphin.'

'Are his eyes that bad?'

'He is almost blind.'

'It is strange,' the old man said. 'He never went turtle-ing. That is what kills the eyes.'

'But you went turtle-ing for years off the Mosquito Coast and your eyes are good.'

'I am a strange old man.'

'But are you strong enough now for a truly big fish?'

'I think so. And there are many tricks.'

'Let us take the stuff home,' the boy said. 'So I can get the cast net and go after the sardines.'

They picked up the gear from the boat. The old man carried the mast on his shoulder and the boy carried the wooden box with the coiled, hard-braided brown lines, the gaff and the harpoon with its shaft. The box with the baits was under the stern of the skiff along with the club that was used to subdue the big fish when they were brought alongside. No one would steal from the old man but it was better to take the sail and the heavy lines home as the dew was bad for them and, though he was quite sure no local people would steal from him, the old man thought that a gaff and a harpoon were needless temptations to leave in a boat.

They walked up the road together to the old man's shack and
went in through its open door. The old man leaned the mast with
its wrapped sail against the wall and the boy put the box and the
other gear beside it. The mast was nearly as long as the one room
of the shack. The shack was made of the tough bud-shields of
the royal palm which are called *guano* and in it there was a bed, a
table, one chair, and a place on the dirt floor to cook with charcoal.
On the brown walls of the flattened, overlapping leaves of the
sturdy fibred *guano* there was a picture in colour of the Sacred
Heart of Jesus and another of the Virgin of Cobre. These were
relics of his wife. Once there had been a tinted photograph of his
wife on the wall but he had taken it down because it made him
too lonely to see it and it was on the shelf in the corner under his
clean shirt.

'What do you have to eat?' the boy asked.

'A pot of yellow rice with fish. Do you want some?'

'No. I will eat at home. Do you want me to make the fire?'

'No. I will make it later on. Or I may eat the rice cold.'

'May I take the cast net?'

'Of course.'

There was no cast net and the boy remembered when they had sold it. But they went through this fiction every day. There was no pot of yellow rice and fish and the boy knew this too.

'Eighty-five is a lucky number,' the old man said. 'How would you like to see me bring one in that dressed out over a thousand pounds?'

'I'll get the cast net and go for sardines. Will you sit in the sun in the doorway?'

'Yes. I have yesterday's paper and I will read the baseball.'

The boy did not know whether yesterday's paper was a fiction too. But the old man brought it out from under the bed.

'Perico gave it to me at the *bodega*,' he explained.

'I'll be back when I have the sardines. I'll keep yours and mine together on ice and we can share them in the morning. When I come back you can tell me about the baseball.'

'The Yankees cannot lose.'

'But I fear the Indians of Cleveland.'

'Have faith in the Yankees my son. Think of the great DiMaggio.'

'I fear both the Tigers of Detroit and the Indians of Cleveland.'

'Be careful or you will fear even the Reds of Cincinnati and the White Sox of Chicago.'

'You study it and tell me when I come back.'

'Do you think we should buy a terminal of the lottery with an eighty-five? Tomorrow is the eighty-fifth day.'

'We can do that,' the boy said. 'But what about the eighty-seven of your great record?'

'It could not happen twice. Do you think you can find an eighty-five?'

'I can order one.'

'One sheet. That's two dollars and a half. Who can we borrow that from?'

'That's easy. I can always borrow two dollars and a half.'

'I think perhaps I can too. But I try not to borrow. First you borrow. Then you beg.'

'Keep warm old man,' the boy said. 'Remember we are in September.'

'The month when the great fish come,' the old man said. 'Anyone can be a fisherman in May.'

'I go now for the sardines,' the boy said.

When the boy came back the old man was asleep in the chair and the sun was down. The boy took the old army blanket off the bed and spread it over the back of the chair and over the old man's shoulders. They were strange shoulders, still powerful although very old, and the neck was still strong too and the creases did not show so much when the old man was asleep and his head fallen forward. His shirt had been patched so many times that it was like the sail and the patches were faded to many different shades by the sun. The old man's head was very old though and with his eyes closed there was no life in his face. The newspaper lay across his knees and the weight of his arm held it there in the evening breeze. He was barefooted.

The boy left him there and when he came back the old man was still asleep.

'Wake up old man,' the boy said and put his hand on one of the old man's knees.

The old man opened his eyes and for a moment he was coming back from a long way away. Then he smiled.

'What have you got?' he asked.

'Supper,' said the boy. 'We're going to have supper.'

'I'm not very hungry.'

'Come on and eat. You can't fish and not eat.'

'I have,' the old man said getting up and taking the newspaper and folding it. Then he started to fold the blanket.

'Keep the blanket around you,' the boy said. 'You'll not fish without eating while I'm alive.'

'Then live a long time and take care of yourself,' the old man said. 'What are we eating?'

'Black beans and rice, fried bananas, and some stew.'

The boy had brought them in a two-decker metal container from the Terrace. The two sets of knives and forks and spoons were in his pocket with a paper napkin wrapped around each set.

'Who gave this to you?'

'Martin. The owner.'

'I must thank him.'

'I thanked him already,' the boy said. 'You don't need to thank him.'

'I'll give him the belly meat of a big fish,' the old man said. 'Has he done this for us more than once?'

'I think so.'

'I must give him something more than the belly meat then. He is very thoughtful for us.'

'He sent two beers.'

'I like the beer in cans best.'

'I know. But this is in bottles, Hatuey beer, and I take back the bottles.'

'That's very kind of you,' the old man said. 'Should we eat?'

'I've been asking you to,' the boy told him gently. 'I have not wished to open the container until you were ready.'

'I'm ready now,' the old man said. 'I only needed time to wash.'

Where did you wash? the boy thought. The village water supply was two streets down the road. I must have water here for him, the boy thought, and soap and a good towel. Why am I so thoughtless? I must get him another shirt and a jacket for the winter and some sort of shoes and another blanket.

'Your stew is excellent,' the old man said.

'Tell me about the baseball,' the boy asked him.

'In the American League it is the Yankees as I said,' the old man said happily.

'They lost today,' the boy told him.

'That means nothing. The great DiMaggio is himself again.'

'They have other men on the team.'

'Naturally. But he makes the difference. In the other league, between Brooklyn and Philadelphia I must take Brooklyn. But then I think of Dick Sisler and those great drives in the old park.'

'There was nothing ever like them. He hits the longest ball I have ever seen.'

'Do you remember when he used to come to the Terrace?' I wanted to take him fishing but I was too timid to ask him. Then I asked you to ask him and you were too timid.'

'I know. It was a great mistake. He might have gone with us. Then we would have that for all of our lives.'

'I would like to take the great DiMaggio fishing,' the old man said. 'They say his father was a fisherman. Maybe he was as poor as we are and would understand.'

'The great Sisler's father was never poor and he, the father, was playing in the big leagues when he was my age.'

'When I was your age I was before the mast on a square-rigged ship that ran to Africa and I have seen lions on the beaches in the evening.'

'I know. You told me.'

'Should we talk about Africa or about baseball?'

'Baseball I think,' the boy said. 'Tell me about the great John J. McGraw.' He said *Jota* for J.

'He used to come to the Terrace sometimes too in the older days. But he was rough and harsh-spoken and difficult when he was drinking. His mind was on horses as well as baseball. At least he carried lists of horses at all times in his pocket and frequently spoke the names of horses on the telephone.'

'He was a great manager,' the boy said. 'My father thinks he was the greatest.'

'Because he came here the most times,' the old man said. 'If Durocher had continued to come here each year your father would think him the greatest manager.'

'Who is the greatest manager, really, Luque or Mike Gonzalez?'

'I think they are equal.'

'And the best fisherman is you.'

'No. I know others better.'

'Què Va,' the boy said. 'There are many good fishermen and some great ones. But there is only you.'

'Thank you. You make me happy. I hope no fish will come along so great that he will prove us wrong.'

'There is no such fish if you are still strong as you say.'

'I may not be as strong as I think,' the old man said. 'But I know many tricks and I have resolution.'

'You ought to go to bed now so that you will be fresh in the morning. I will take the things back to the Terrace.'

'Good night then. I will wake you in the morning.'

'You're my alarm clock,' the boy said.

'Age is my alarm clock,' the old man said. 'Why do old men wake so early? Is it to have one longer day?'

'I don't know,' the boy said. 'All I know is that young boys sleep late and hard.'

'I can remember it,' the old man said. 'I'll waken you in time.'

'I do not like for him to waken me. It is as though I were inferior.'

'I know.'

'Sleep well old man.'

The boy went out. They had eaten with no light on the table and the old man took off his trousers and went to bed in the dark. He rolled his trousers up to make a pillow, putting the newspaper inside them. He rolled himself in the blanket and slept on the other old newspapers that covered the springs of the bed.

He was asleep in a short time and he dreamed of Africa when he was a boy and the long, golden beaches and the white beaches, so white they hurt your eyes, and the high capes and the great brown mountains. He lived along that coast now every night and in his dreams he heard the surf roar and saw the native boats come riding through it. He smelled the tar and oakum of the deck as he slept and he smelled the smell of Africa that the land breeze brought at morning.

Usually when he smelled the land breeze he woke up and dressed to go and wake the boy. But tonight the smell of the land breeze came very early and he knew it was too early in his dream and went on dreaming to see the white peaks of the Islands rising from the sea and then he dreamed of the different harbours and roadsteads of the Canary Islands.

He no longer dreamed of storms, nor of women, nor of great occurrences, nor of great fish, nor fights, nor contests of strength, nor of his wife. He only dreamed of places now and of the lions on the beach. They played like young cats in the dusk and he loved them as he loved the boy. He never dreamed about the boy. He simply woke, looked out the open door at the moon and unrolled his trousers and put them on. He urinated outside the shack and then went up the road to wake the boy. He was shivering with the morning cold. But he knew he would shiver himself warm and that soon he would be rowing.

The door of the house where the boy lived was unlocked and he opened it and walked in quietly with his bare feet. The boy was asleep on a cot in the first room and the old man could see him clearly with the light that came in from the dying moon. He took hold of one foot gently and held it until the boy woke and turned and looked at him. The old man nodded and the boy took his trousers from the chair by the bed and, sitting on the bed, pulled them on.

The old man went out the door and the boy came after him. He was sleepy and the old man put his arm across his shoulders and said, 'I am sorry.'

'Què Va,' the boy said. 'It is what a man must do.'

They walked down the road to the old man's shack and all along the road, in the dark, barefoot men were moving, carrying the masts of their boats.

When they reached the old man's shack the boy took the rolls of line in the basket and the harpoon and gaff and the old man carried the mast with the furled sail on his shoulder.

'Do you want coffee?' the boy asked.

'We'll put the gear in the boat and then get some.'

They had coffee from condensed-milk cans at an early morning place that served fishermen.

'How did you sleep old man?' the boy asked. He was waking up now although it was still hard for him to leave his sleep.

'Very well, Manolin,' the old man said. 'I feel confident today.'

'So do I,' the boy said. 'Now I must get your sardines and mine and your fresh baits. He brings our gear himself. He never wants anyone to carry anything.'

'We're different,' the old man said. 'I let you carry things when you were five years old.'

'I know it,' the boy said. 'I'll be right back. Have another coffee. We have credit here.'

He walked off, barefooted on the coral rocks, to the ice house where the baits were stored.

The old man drank his coffee slowly. It was all he would have all day and he knew that he should take it. For a long time now eating had bored him and he never carried a lunch. He had a bottle of water in the bow of the skiff and that was all he needed for the day.

The boy was back now with the sardines and the two baits wrapped in a newspaper and they went down the trail to the skiff, feeling the pebbled sand under their feet, and lifted the skiff and slid her into the water.

'Good luck old man.'

'Good luck,' the old man said. He fitted the rope lashings of the oars onto the thole pins and, leaning forward against the thrust of the blades in the water, he began to row out of the harbour in the dark. There were other boats from the other beaches going out to sea and the old man heard the dip and push of their oars even though he could not see them now the moon was below the hills.

Sometimes someone would speak in a boat. But most of the boats were silent except for the dip of the oars. They spread apart after they were out of the mouth of the harbour and each one headed for the part of the ocean where he hoped to find fish. The old man knew he was going far out and he left the smell of the land behind and rowed out into the clean early morning smell of the ocean. He saw the phosphorescence of the Gulf weed in the water as he rowed over the part of the ocean that the fishermen called the great well because there was a sudden deep of seven hundred fathoms where all sorts of fish congregated because of the swirl the current made against the steep walls of the floor of the ocean. Here there were concentrations of shrimp and bait fish and sometimes schools of squid in the deepest holes and these rose close to the surface at night where all the wandering fish fed on them.

In the dark the old man could feel the morning coming and as he rowed he heard the trembling sound as flying fish left the water and the hissing that their stiff set wings made as they soared away in the darkness. He was very fond of flying fish as they were his principal friends on the ocean. He was sorry for the birds, especially the small delicate dark terns that were always flying and looking and almost never finding, and he thought, 'The birds have a harder life than we do except for the robber birds and the heavy strong ones. Why did they make birds so delicate and fine as those sea swallows when the ocean can be so cruel? She is kind and very beautiful. But she can be so cruel and it comes so suddenly and such birds that fly, dipping and hunting, with their small sad voices are made too delicately for the sea.'

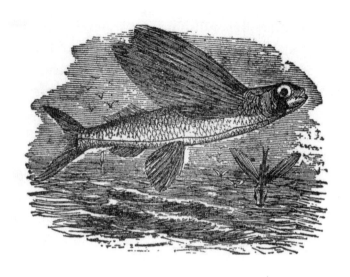

He always thought of the sea as *la mar* which is what people call her in Spanish when they love her. Sometimes those who love her say bad things of her but they are always said as though she were a woman. Some of the younger fishermen, those who used buoys as floats for their lines and had motorboats, bought when the shark livers had brought much money, spoke of her as *el mar* which is masculine. They spoke of her as a contestant or a place or even an enemy. But the old man always thought of her as feminine and as something that gave or withheld great favours, and if she did wild or wicked things it was because she could not help them. The moon affects her as it does a woman, he thought.

He was rowing steadily and it was no effort for him since he kept well within his speed and the surface of the ocean was flat except for the occasional swirls of the current. He was letting the current do a third of the work and as it started to be light he saw he was already further out than he had hoped to be at this hour.

I worked the deep wells for a week and did nothing, he thought. Today I'll work out where the schools of bonito and albacore are and maybe there will be a big one with them.

Before it was really light he had his baits out and was drifting with the current. One bait was down forty fathoms. The second was at seventy-five and the third and fourth were down in the blue water at one hundred and one hundred and twenty-five fathoms. Each bait hung head down with the shank of the hook inside the bait fish, tied and sewed solid, and all the projecting part of the hook, the curve and the point, was covered with fresh sardines. Each sardine was hooked through both eyes so that they made a half-garland on the projecting steel. There was no part of the hook that a great fish could feel which was not sweet-smelling and good-tasting.

The boy had given him two fresh small tunas, or albacores, which hung on the two deepest lines like plummets and, on the others, he had a big blue runner and a yellow jack that had been used before; but they were in good condition still and had the excellent sardines to give them scent and attractiveness. Each line, as thick around as a big pencil, was looped onto a green-sapped stick so that any pull or touch on the bait would make the stick dip and each line had two forty-fathom coils which could be made fast to the other spare coils so that, if it were necessary, a fish could take out over three hundred fathoms of line.

Now the man watched the dip of the three sticks over the side of the skiff and rowed gently to keep the lines straight up and down and at their proper depths. It was quite light and any moment now the sun would rise.

The sun rose thinly from the sea and the old man could see the other boats, low on the water and well in toward the shore, spread out across the current. Then the sun was brighter and the glare came on the water and then, as it rose clear, the flat sea sent it back at his eyes so that it hurt sharply and he rowed without looking into it. He looked down into the water and watched the lines that went straight down into the dark of the water. He kept them straighter than anyone did, so that at each level in the darkness of the stream there would be a bait waiting exactly where he wished it to be for any fish that swam there. Others let them drift with the current and sometimes they were at sixty fathoms when the fishermen thought they were at a hundred.

But, he thought, I keep them with precision. Only I have no luck any more. But who knows? Maybe today. Every day is a new day. It is better to be lucky. But I would rather be exact. Then when luck comes you are ready.

The sun was two hours higher now and it did not hurt his eyes so much to look into the east. There were only three boats in sight now and they showed very low and far inshore.

All my life the early sun has hurt my eyes, he thought. Yet they are still good. In the evening I can look straight into it without getting the blackness. It has more force in the evening too. But in the morning it is painful.

Just then he saw a man-of-war bird with his long black wings circling in the sky ahead of him. He made a quick drop, slanting down on his back-swept wings, and then circled again.

'He's got something,' the old man said aloud. 'He's not just looking.'

He rowed slowly and steadily toward where the bird was circling. He did not hurry and he kept his lines straight up and down. But he crowded the current a little so that he was still fishing correctly though faster than he would have fished if he was not trying to use the bird.

The bird went higher in the air and circled again, his wings motionless. Then he dove suddenly and the old man saw flying fish spurt out of the water and sail desperately over the surface.

'Dolphin,' the old man said aloud. 'Big dolphin.'

He shipped his oars and brought a small line from under the bow. It had a wire leader and a medium-sized hook and he baited it with one of the sardines. He let it go over the side and then made it fast to a ring bolt in the stern. Then he baited another line and left it coiled in the shade of the bow. He went back to rowing and to watching the long-winged black bird who was working, now, low over the water.

As he watched the bird dipped again slanting his wings for the dive and then swinging them wildly and ineffectually as he followed the flying fish. The old man could see the slight bulge in the water that the big dolphin raised as they followed the escaping fish. The dolphin were cutting through the water below the flight of the fish and would be in the water, driving at speed, when the fish dropped. It is a big school of dolphin, he thought. They are wide spread and the flying fish have little chance. The bird has no chance. The flying fish are too big for him and they go too fast.

He watched the flying fish burst out again and again and the ineffectual movements of the bird. That school has gotten away from me, he thought. They are moving out too fast and too far. But perhaps I will pick up a stray and perhaps my big fish is around them. My big fish must be somewhere.

The clouds over the land now rose like mountains and the coast was only a long green line with the gray-blue hills behind it. The water was a dark blue now, so dark that it was almost purple. As he looked down into it he saw the red sifting of the plankton in the dark water and the strange light the sun made now. He watched his lines to see them go straight down out of sight into the water and he was happy to see so much plankton because it meant fish. The strange light the sun made in the water, now that the sun was higher, meant good weather and so did the shape of the clouds over the land. But the bird was almost out of sight now and nothing showed on the surface of the water but some patches of yellow, sun-bleached Sargasso weed and the purple, formalized, iridescent, gelatinous bladder of a Portuguese man-of-war floating close beside the boat. It turned on its side and then righted itself. It floated cheerfully as a bubble with its long deadly purple filaments trailing a yard behind it in the water.

'*Agua mala*,' the man said. 'You whore.'

From where he swung lightly against his oars he looked down into the water and saw the tiny fish that were coloured like the trailing filaments and swam between them and under the small shade the bubble made as it drifted. They were immune to its poison. But men were not and when some of the filaments would catch on a line and rest there slimy and purple while the old man was working a fish, he would have welts and sores on his arms and hands of the sort that poison ivy or poison oak can give. But these poisonings from the *agua mala* came quickly and struck like a whiplash.

The iridescent bubbles were beautiful. But they were the falsest thing in the sea and the old man loved to see the big sea turtles eating them. The turtles saw them, approached them from the front, then shut their eyes so they were completely carapaced and ate them filaments and all. The old man loved to see the turtles eat them and he loved to walk on them on the beach after a storm and hear them pop when he stepped on them with the horny soles of his feet.

He loved green turtles and hawks-bills with their elegance and speed and their great value and he had a friendly contempt for the huge, stupid logger-heads, yellow in their armor-plating, strange in their love-making, and happily eating the Portuguese men-of-war with their eyes shut.

He had no mysticism about turtles although he had gone in turtle boats for many years. He was sorry for them all, even the great trunk-backs that were as long as the skiff and weighed a ton. Most people are heartless about turtles because a turtle's heart will beat for hours after he has been cut up and butchered. But the old man thought, I have such a heart too and my feet and hands are like theirs. He ate the white eggs to give himself strength. He ate them all through May to be strong in September and October for the truly big fish.

He also drank a cup of shark liver oil each day from the big drum in the shack where many of the fishermen kept their gear. It was there for all fishermen who wanted it. Most fishermen hated the taste. But it was no worse than getting up at the hours that they rose and it was very good against all colds and grippes and it was good for the eyes.

Now the old man looked up and saw that the bird was circling again.

'He's found fish,' he said aloud. No flying fish broke the surface and there was no scattering of bait fish. But as the old man watched, a small tuna rose in the air, turned and dropped head first into the water. The tuna shone silver in the sun and after he had dropped back into the water another and another rose and they were jumping in all directions, churning the water and leaping in long jumps after the bait. They were circling it and driving it.

If they don't travel too fast I will get into them, the old man thought, and he watched the school working the water white and the bird now dropping and dipping into the bait fish that were forced to the surface in their panic.

'The bird is a great help,' the old man said. Just then the stern line came taut under his foot, where he had kept a loop of the line, and he dropped his oars and felt the weight of the small tuna's shivering pull as he held the line firm and commenced to haul it in. The shivering increased as he pulled in and he could see the blue back of the fish in the water and the gold of his sides before he swung him over the side and into the boat. He lay in the stern in the sun, compact and bullet-shaped, his big, unintelligent eyes staring as he thumped his life out against the planking of the boat with the quick shivering strokes of his neat, fast-moving tail. The old man hit him on the head for kindness and kicked him, his body still shuddering, under the shade of the stern.

'Albacore,' he said aloud. 'He'll make a beautiful bait. He'll weigh ten pounds.'

He did not remember when he had first started to talk aloud when he was by himself. He had sung when he was by himself in the old days and he had sung at night sometimes when he was alone steering on his watch in the smacks or in the turtle boats. He had probably started to talk aloud, when alone, when the boy had left. But he did not remember. When he and the boy fished together they usually spoke only when it was necessary. They talked at night or when they were storm-bound by bad weather. It was considered a virtue not to talk unnecessarily at sea and the old man had always considered it so and respected it. But now he said his thoughts aloud many times since there was no one that they could annoy.

'If the others heard me talking out loud they would think that I am crazy,' he said aloud. 'But since I am not crazy, I do not care. And the rich have radios to talk to them in their boats and to bring them the baseball.'

Now is no time to think of baseball, he thought. Now is the time to think of only one thing. That which I was born for. There might be a big one around that school, he thought. I picked up only a straggler from the albacore that were feeding. But they are working far out and fast. Everything that shows on the surface today travels very fast and to the north-east. Can that be the time of day? Or is it some sign of weather that I do not know?

He could not see the green of the shore now but only the tops of the blue hills that showed white as though they were snow-capped and the clouds that looked like high snow mountains above them. The sea was very dark and the light made prisms in the water. The myriad flecks of the plankton were annulled now by the high sun and it was only the great deep prisms in the blue water that the old man saw now with his lines going straight down into the water that was a mile deep.

The tuna, the fishermen called all the fish of that species tuna and only distinguished among them by their proper names when they came to sell them or to trade them for baits, were down again. The sun was hot now and the old man felt it on the back of his neck and felt the sweat trickle down his back as he rowed.

I could just drift, he thought, and sleep and put a bight of line around my toe to wake me. But today is eighty-five days and I should fish the day well.

Just then, watching his lines, he saw one of the projecting green sticks dip sharply.

'Yes,' he said. 'Yes,' and shipped his oars without bumping the boat. He reached out for the line and held it softly between the thumb and forefinger of his right hand. He felt no strain nor weight and he held the line lightly. Then it came again. This time it was a tentative pull, not solid nor heavy, and he knew exactly what it was. One hundred fathoms down a marlin was eating the sardines that covered the point and the shank of the hook where the hand-forged hook projected from the head of the small tuna.

The old man held the line delicately, and softly, with his left hand, unleashed it from the stick. Now he could let it run through his fingers without the fish feeling any tension.

This far out, he must be huge in this month, he thought. Eat them, fish. Eat them. Please eat them. How fresh they are and you down there six hundred feet in that cold water in the dark. Make another turn in the dark and come back and eat them.

He felt the light delicate pulling and then a harder pull when a sardine's head must have been more difficult to break from the hook. Then there was nothing.

'Come on,' the old man said aloud. 'Make another turn. Just smell them. Aren't they lovely? Eat them good now and then there is the tuna. Hard and cold and lovely. Don't be shy, fish. Eat them.'

He waited with the line between his thumb and his finger, watching it and the other lines at the same time for the fish might have swum up or down. Then came the same delicate pulling touch again.

'He'll take it,' the old man said aloud. 'God help him to take it.'

He did not take it though. He was gone and the old man felt nothing.

'He can't have gone,' he said. 'Christ knows he can't have gone. He's making a turn. Maybe he has been hooked before and he remembers something of it.'

Then he felt the gentle touch on the line and he was happy.

'It was only his turn,' he said. 'He'll take it.'

He was happy feeling the gentle pulling and then he felt something hard and unbelievably heavy. It was the weight of the fish and he let the line slip down, down, down, unrolling off the first of the two reserve coils. As it went down, slipping lightly through the old man's fingers, he still could feel the great weight, though the pressure of his thumb and finger were almost imperceptible.

'What a fish,' he said. 'He has it sideways in his mouth now and he is moving off with it.'

Then he will turn and swallow it, he thought. He did not say that because he knew that if you said a good thing it might not happen. He knew what a huge fish this was and he thought of him moving away in the darkness with the tuna held crosswise in his mouth. At that moment he felt him stop moving but the weight was still there. Then the weight increased and he gave more line. He tightened the pressure of his thumb and finger for a moment and the weight increased and was going straight down.

'He's taken it,' he said. 'Now I'll let him eat it well.'

He let the line slip through his fingers while he reached down with his left hand and made fast the free end of the two reserve coils to the loop of the two reserve coils of the next line. Now he was ready. He had three forty-fathom coils of line in reserve now, as well as the coil he was using.

'Eat it a little more,' he said. 'Eat it well.'

Eat it so that the point of the hook goes into your heart and kills you, he thought. Come up easy and let me put the harpoon into you. All right. Are you ready? Have you been long enough at table?

'Now!' he said aloud and struck hard with both hands, gained a yard of line and then struck again and again, swinging with each arm alternately on the cord with all the strength of his arms and the pivoted weight of his body.

Nothing happened. The fish just moved away slowly and the old man could not raise him an inch. His line was strong and made for heavy fish and he held it against his back until it was so taut that beads of water were jumping from it. Then it began to make a slow hissing sound in the water and he still held it, bracing himself against the thwart and leaning back against the pull. The boat began to move slowly off toward the north-west.

The fish moved steadily and they travelled slowly on the calm water. The other baits were still in the water but there was nothing to be done.

'I wish I had the boy,' the old man said aloud. 'I'm being towed by a fish and I'm the towing bitt. I could make the line fast. But then he could break it. I must hold him all I can and give him line when he must have it. Thank God he is travelling and not going down.'

What I will do if he decides to go down, I don't know. What I'll do if he sounds and dies I don't know. But I'll do something. There are plenty of things I can do.

He held the line against his back and watched its slant in the water and the skiff moving steadily to the north-west.

This will kill him, the old man thought. He can't do this for ever. But four hours later the fish was still swimming steadily out to sea, towing the skiff, and the old man was still braced solidly with the line across his back.

'It was noon when I hooked him,' he said. 'And I have never seen him.'

He had pushed his straw hat hard down on his head before he hooked the fish and it was cutting his forehead. He was thirsty too and he got down on his knees and, being careful not to jerk on the line, moved as far into the bow as he could get and reached the water bottle with one hand. He opened it and drank a little. Then he rested against the bow. He rested sitting on the unstepped mast and sail and tried not to think but only to endure.

Then he looked behind him and saw that no land was visible. That makes no difference, he thought. I can always come in on the glow from Havana. There are two more hours before the sun sets and maybe he will come up before that. If he doesn't maybe he will come up with the moon. If he does not do that maybe he will come up with the sunrise. I have no cramps and I feel strong. It is he that has the hook in his mouth. But what a fish to pull like that. He must have his mouth shut tight on the wire. I wish I could see him. I wish I could see him only once to know what I have against me.

The fish never changed his course nor his direction all that night as far as the man could tell from watching the stars. It was cold after the sun went down and the old man's sweat dried cold on his back and his arms and his old legs. During the day he had taken the sack that covered the bait box and spread it in the sun to dry. After the sun went down he tied it around his neck so that it hung down over his back and he cautiously worked it down under the line that was across his shoulders now. The sack cushioned the line and he had found a way of leaning forward against the bow so that he was almost comfortable. The position actually was only somewhat less intolerable; but he thought of it as almost comfortable.

I can do nothing with him and he can do nothing with me, he thought. Not as long as he keeps this up.

Once he stood up and urinated over the side of the skiff and looked at the stars and checked his course. The line showed like a phosphorescent streak in the water straight out from his shoulders. They were moving more slowly now and the glow of Havana was not so strong, so that he knew the current must be carrying them to the eastward. If I lose the glare of Havana we must be going more to the eastward, he thought. For if the fish's course held true I must see it for many more hours. I wonder how the baseball came out in the grand leagues today, he thought. It would be wonderful to do this with a radio. Then he thought, think of it always. Think of what you are doing. You must do nothing stupid.

Then he said aloud, 'I wish I had the boy. To help me and to see this.'

No one should be alone in their old age, he thought. But it is unavoidable. I must remember to eat the tuna before he spoils in order to keep strong. Remember, no matter how little you want to, that you must eat him in the morning. Remember, he said to himself.

During the night two porpoises came around the boat and he could hear them rolling and blowing. He could tell the difference between the blowing noise the male made and the sighing blow of the female.

'They are good,' he said. 'They play and make jokes and love one another. They are our brothers like the flying fish.'

Then he began to pity the great fish that he had hooked. He is wonderful and strange and who knows how old he is, he thought. Never have I had such a strong fish nor one who acted so strangely. Perhaps he is too wise to jump. He could ruin me by jumping or by a wild rush. But perhaps he has been hooked many times before and he knows that this is how he should make his fight. He cannot know that it is only one man against him, nor that it is an old man. But what a great fish he is and what will he bring in the market if the flesh is good. He took the bait like a male and he pulls like a male and his fight has no panic in it. I wonder if he has any plans or if he is just as desperate as I am?

He remembered the time he had hooked one of a pair of marlin. The male fish always let the female fish feed first and the hooked fish, the female, made a wild, panic-stricken, despairing fight that soon exhausted her, and all the time the male had stayed with her, crossing the line and circling with her on the surface. He had stayed so close that the old man was afraid he would cut the line with his tail which was sharp as a scythe and almost of that size and shape. When the old man had gaffed her and clubbed her, holding the rapier bill with its sandpaper edge and clubbing her across the top of her head until her colour turned to a colour almost like the backing of mirrors, and then, with the boy's aid, hoisted her aboard, the male fish had stayed by the side of the boat. Then, while the old man was clearing the lines and preparing the harpoon, the male fish jumped high into the air beside the boat to see where the female was and then went down deep, his lavender wings, that were his pectoral fins, spread wide and all his wide lavender stripes showing. He was beautiful, the old man remembered, and he had stayed.

That was the saddest thing I ever saw with them, the old man thought. The boy was sad too and we begged her pardon and butchered her promptly.

'I wish the boy was here,' he said aloud and settled himself against the rounded planks of the bow and felt the strength of the great fish through the line he held across his shoulders moving steadily toward whatever he had chosen.

When once, through my treachery, it had been necessary to him to make a choice, the old man thought.

His choice had been to stay in the deep dark water far out beyond all snares and traps and treacheries. My choice was to go there to find him beyond all people. Beyond all people in the world. Now we are joined together and have been since noon. And no one to help either one of us.

Perhaps I should not have been a fisherman, he thought. But

that was the thing that I was born for. I must surely remember to eat the tuna after it gets light.

Some time before daylight something took one of the baits that were behind him. He heard the stick break and the line begin to rush out over the gunwale of the skiff. In the darkness he loosened his sheath knife and taking all the strain of the fish on his left shoulder he leaned back and cut the line against the wood of the gunwale. Then he cut the other line closest to him and in the dark made the loose ends of the reserve coils fast. He worked skillfully with the one hand and put his foot on the coils to hold them as he drew his knots tight. Now he had six reserve coils of line. There were two from each bait he had severed and the two from the bait the fish had taken and they were all connected.

After it is light, he thought, I will work back to the forty-fathom bait and cut it away too and link up the reserve coils. I will have lost two hundred fathoms of good Catalan *cardel* and the hooks and leaders. That can be replaced. But who replaces this fish if I hook some fish and it cuts him off? I don't know what that fish was that took the bait just now. It could have been a marlin or a broadbill or a shark. I never felt him. I had to get rid of him too fast.

Aloud he said, 'I wish I had the boy.'

But you haven't got the boy, he thought. You have only yourself and you had better work back to the last line now, in the dark or not in the dark, and cut it away and hook up the two reserve coils.

So he did it. It was difficult in the dark and once the fish made a surge that pulled him down on his face and made a cut below his eye. The blood ran down his cheek a little way. But it coagulated and dried before it reached his chin and he worked his way back to the bow and rested against the wood. He adjusted the sack and carefully worked the line so that it came across a new part of his shoulders and, holding it anchored with his shoulders, he carefully felt the pull of the fish and then felt with his hand the progress of the skiff through the water.

I wonder what he made that lurch for, he thought. The wire must have slipped on the great hill of his back. Certainly his back cannot feel as badly as mine does. But he cannot pull this skiff for ever, no matter how great he is. Now everything is cleared away that might make trouble and I have a big reserve of line; all that a man can ask.

'Fish,' he said softly, aloud, 'I'll stay with you until I am dead.'

He'll stay with me too, I suppose, the old man thought and he waited for it to be light. It was cold now in the time before daylight and he pushed against the wood to be warm. I can do it as long as he can, he thought. And in the first light the line extended out and down into the water. The boat moved steadily and when the first edge of the sun rose it was on the old man's right shoulder.

'He's headed north,' the old man said. The current will have set us far to the eastward, he thought. I wish he would turn with the current. That would show that he was tiring.

When the sun had risen further the old man realized that the fish was not tiring. There was only one favourable sign. The slant of the line showed he was swimming at a lesser depth. That did not necessarily mean that he would jump. But he might.

'God let him jump,' the old man said. 'I have enough line to handle him.'

Maybe if I can increase the tension just a little it will hurt him and he will jump, he thought. Now that it is daylight let him jump so that he'll fill the sacs along his backbone with air and then he cannot go deep to die.

He tried to increase the tension, but the line had been taut up to the very edge of the breaking point since he had hooked the fish and he felt the harshness as he leaned back to pull and knew he could put no more strain on it. I must not jerk it ever, he thought. Each jerk widens the cut the hook makes and then when he does jump he might throw it. Anyway I feel better with the sun and for once I do not have to look into it.

There was yellow weed on the line but the old man knew that only made an added drag and he was pleased. It was the yellow Gulf weed that had made so much phosphorescence in the night.

'Fish,' he said, 'I love you and respect you very much. But I will kill you dead before this day ends.'

Let us hope so, he thought.

A small bird came toward the skiff from the north. He was a warbler and flying very low over the water. The old man could see that he was very tired.

The bird made the stern of the boat and rested there. Then he flew around the old man's head and rested on the line where he was more comfortable.

'How old are you?' the old man asked the bird. 'Is this your first trip?'

The bird looked at him when he spoke. He was too tired even to examine the line and he teetered on it as his delicate feet gripped it fast.

'It's steady,' the old man told him. 'It's too steady. You shouldn't be that tired after a windless night. What are birds coming to?'

The hawks, he thought, that come out to sea to meet them. But he said nothing of this to the bird who could not understand him anyway and who would learn about the hawks soon enough.

'Take a good rest, small bird,' he said. 'Then go in and take your chance like any man or bird or fish.'

It encouraged him to talk because his back had stiffened in the night and it hurt truly now.

'Stay at my house if you like, bird,' he said. 'I am sorry I cannot hoist the sail and take you in with the small breeze that is rising. But I am with a friend.'

Just then the fish gave a sudden lurch that pulled the old man down on to the bow and would have pulled him overboard if he had not braced himself and given some line.

The bird had flown up when the line jerked and the old man had not even seen him go. He felt the line carefully with his right hand and noticed his hand was bleeding.

'Something hurt him then,' he said aloud and pulled back on the line to see if he could turn the fish. But when he was touching the breaking point he held steady and settled back against the strain of the line.

'You're feeling it now, fish,' he said. 'And so, God knows, am I.'

He looked around for the bird now because he would have liked him for company. The bird was gone.

You did not stay long, the man thought. But it is rougher where you are going until you make the shore. How did I let the fish cut me with that one quick pull he made? I must be getting very stupid. Or perhaps I was looking at the small bird and thinking of him. Now I will pay attention to my work and then I must eat the tuna so that I will not have a failure of strength.

'I wish the boy were here and that I had some salt,' he said aloud.

Shifting the weight of the line to his left shoulder and kneeling carefully he washed his hand in the ocean and held it there, submerged, for more than a minute watching the blood trail away and the steady movement of the water against his hand as the boat moved.

'He has slowed much,' he said.

The old man would have liked to keep his hand in the salt water longer but he was afraid of another sudden lurch by the fish and he stood up and braced himself and held his hand up against the sun. It was only a line burn that had cut his flesh. But it was in the working part of his hand. He knew he would need his hands before this was over and he did not like to be cut before it started.

'Now,' he said, when his hand had dried, 'I must eat the small tuna. I can reach him with the gaff and eat him here in comfort.'

He knelt down and found the tuna under the stem with the gaff and drew it toward him keeping it clear of the coiled lines. Holding the line with his left shoulder again, and bracing on his left hand and arm, he took the tuna off the gaff hook and put the gaff back in place. He put one knee on the fish and cut strips of dark red meat longitudinally from the back of the head to the tail. They were wedge-shaped strips and he cut them from next to the backbone down to the edge of the belly. When he had cut six strips he spread them out on the wood of the bow, wiped his knife on his trousers, and lifted the carcass of the bonito by the tail and dropped it overboard.

'I don't think I can eat an entire one,' he said and drew his knife across one of the strips. He could feel the steady hard pull of the line and his left hand was cramped. It drew up tight on the heavy cord and he looked at it in disgust.

'What kind of a hand is that,' he said. 'Cramp then if you want. Make yourself into a claw. It will do you no good.'

Come on, he thought and looked down into the dark water at the slant of the line. Eat it now and it will strengthen the hand. It is not the hand's fault and you have been many hours with the fish. But you can stay with him for ever. Eat the bonito now.

He picked up a piece and put it in his mouth and chewed it slowly. It was not unpleasant.

Chew it well, he thought, and get all the juices. It would not be had to eat with a little lime or with lemon or with salt.

'How do you feel, hand?' he asked the cramped hand that was almost as stiff as rigor mortis. 'I'll eat some more for you.'

He ate the other part of the piece that he had cut in two. He chewed it carefully and then spat out the skin.

'How does it go, hand? Or is it too early to know?'

He took another full piece and chewed it.

'It is a strong full-blooded fish,' he thought. 'I was lucky to get him instead of dolphin. Dolphin is too sweet. This is hardly sweet at all and all the strength is still in it.'

There is no sense in being anything but practical though, he thought. I wish I had some salt. And I do not know whether the sun will rot or dry what is left, so I had better eat it all although I am not hungry. The fish is calm and steady. I will eat it all and then I will be ready.

'Be patient, hand,' he said. 'I do this for you.'

I wish I could feed the fish, he thought. He is my brother. But I must kill him and keep strong to do it. Slowly and conscientiously he ate all of the wedge-shaped strips of fish.

He straightened up, wiping his hand on his trousers.

'Now,' he said. 'You can let the cord go, hand, and I will handle him with the right arm alone until you stop that nonsense.' He put his left foot on the heavy line that the left hand had held and lay back against the pull against his back.

'God help me to have the cramp go,' he said. 'Because I do not know what the fish is going to do.'

But he seems calm, he thought, and following his plan. But what is his plan, he thought. And what is mine? Mine I must improvise to his because of his great size. If he will jump I can kill him. But he stays down for ever. Then I will stay down with him for ever.

He rubbed the cramped hand against his trousers and tried to gentle the fingers. But it would not open. Maybe it will open with the sun, he thought. Maybe it will open when the strong raw tuna is digested. If I have to have it, I will open it, cost whatever it costs. But I do not want to open it now by force. Let it open by itself and come back of its own accord. After all I abused it much in the night when it was necessary to free and untie the various lines.

He looked across the sea and knew how alone he was now. But he could see the prisms in the deep dark water and the line stretching ahead and the strange undulation of the calm. The clouds were building up now for the trade wind and he looked ahead and saw a flight of wild ducks etching themselves against the sky over the water, then blurring, then etching again and he knew no man was ever alone on the sea.

He thought of how some men feared being out of sight of land in a small boat and knew they were right in the months of sudden bad weather. But now they were in hurricane months and, when there are no hurricanes, the weather of hurricane months is the best of all the year.

If there is a hurricane you always see the signs of it in the sky for days ahead, if you are at sea. They do not see it ashore because they do not know what to look for, he thought. The land must make a difference too, in the shape of the clouds. But we have no hurricane coming now.

He looked at the sky and saw the white cumulus built like friendly piles of ice cream and high above were the thin feathers of the cirrus against the high September sky.

'Light *brisa*,' he said. 'Better weather for me than for you, fish.'

His left hand was still cramped, but he was unknotting it slowly.

I hate a cramp, he thought. It is a treachery of one's own body. It is humiliating before others to have a diarrhoea from ptomaine poisoning or to vomit from it. But a cramp, he thought of it as a *calambre*, humiliates oneself especially when one is alone.

If the boy were here he could rub it for me and loosen it down from the forearm, he thought. But it will loosen up.

Then, with his right hand he felt the difference in the pull of the line before he saw the slant change in the water. Then, as he leaned against the line and slapped his left hand hard and fast against his thigh he saw the line slanting slowly upward.

'He's coming up,' he said. 'Come on hand. Please come on.'

The line rose slowly and steadily and then the surface of the ocean bulged ahead of the boat and the fish came out. He came out unendingly and water poured from his sides. He was bright in the sun and his head and back were dark purple and in the sun the stripes on his sides showed wide and a light lavender. His sword was as long as a baseball bat and tapered like a rapier and he rose his full length from the water and then re-entered it, smoothly, like a diver and the old man saw the great scythe-blade of his tail go under and the line commenced to race out.

'He is two feet longer than the skiff,' the old man said. The line was going out fast but steadily and the fish was not panicked. The old man was trying with both hands to keep the line just inside of breaking strength. He knew that if he could not slow the fish with a steady pressure the fish could take out all the line and break it.

He is a great fish and I must convince him, he thought. I must never let him learn his strength nor what he could do if he made his run. If I were him I would put in everything now and go until something broke. But, thank God, they are not as intelligent as we who kill them; although they are more noble and more able.

The old man had seen many great fish. He had seen many that

weighed more than a thousand pounds and he had caught two of that size in his life, but never alone. Now alone, and out of sight of land, he was fast to the biggest fish that he had ever seen and bigger than he had ever heard of, and his left hand was still as tight as the gripped claws of an eagle.

It will uncramp though, he thought. Surely it will uncramp to help my right hand. There are three things that are brothers: the fish and my two hands. It must uncramp. It is unworthy of it to be cramped. The fish had slowed again and was going at his usual pace.

I wonder why he jumped, the old man thought. He jumped almost as though to show me how big he was. I know now, anyway, he thought. I wish I could show him what sort of man I am. But then he would see the cramped hand. Let him think I am more man than I am and I will be so. I wish I was the fish, he thought, with everything he has against only my will and my intelligence.

He settled comfortably against the wood and took his suffering as it came and the fish swam steadily and the boat moved slowly through the dark water. There was a small sea rising with the wind coming up from the east and at noon the old man's left hand was uncramped.

'Bad news for you, fish,' he said and shifted the line over the sacks that covered his shoulders.

He was comfortable but suffering, although he did not admit the suffering at all.

'I am not religious,' he said. 'But I will say ten Our Fathers and ten Hail Marys that I should catch this fish, and I promise to make a pilgrimage to the Virgin of Cobre if I catch him. That is a promise.'

He commenced to say his prayers mechanically. Sometimes he would be so tired that he could not remember the prayer and then he would say them fast so that they would come automatically. Hail Marys are easier to say than Our Fathers, he thought.

'Hail Mary full of Grace the Lord is with thee. Blessed art thou among women and blessed is the fruit of thy womb, Jesus. Holy Mary, Mother of God, pray for us sinners now and at the hour of our death. Amen.' Then he added, 'Blessed Virgin, pray for the death of this fish. Wonderful though he is.'

With his prayers said, and feeling much better, but suffering exactly as much, and perhaps a little more, he leaned against the wood of the bow and began, mechanically, to work the fingers of his left hand.

The sun was hot now although the breeze was rising gently.

'I had better re-bait that little line out over the stern,' he said. 'If the fish decides to stay another night I will need to eat again and the water is low in the bottle. I don't think I can get anything but a dolphin here. But if I eat him fresh enough he won't be bad. I wish a flying fish would come on board tonight. But I have no light to attract them. A flying fish is excellent to eat raw and I would not have to cut him up. I must save all my strength now. Christ, I did not know he was so big.'

'I'll kill him though,' he said. 'In all his greatness and his glory.'

Although it is unjust, he thought. But I will show him what a man can do and what a man endures.

'I told the boy I was a strange old man,' he said. 'Now is when I must prove it.'

The thousand times that he had proved it meant nothing. Now

he was proving it again. Each time was a new time and he never thought about the past when he was doing it.

I wish he'd sleep and I could sleep and dream about the lions, he thought. Why are the lions the main thing that is left? Don't think, old man, he said to himself. Rest gently now against the wood and think of nothing. He is working. Work as little as you can.

It was getting into the afternoon and the boat still moved slowly and steadily. But there was an added drag now from the easterly breeze and the old man rode gently with the small sea and the hurt of the cord across his back came to him easily and smoothly.

Once in the afternoon the line started to rise again. But the fish only continued to swim at a slightly higher level. The sun was on the old man's left arm and shoulder and on his back. So he knew the fish had turned east of north.

Now that he had seen him once, he could picture the fish swimming in the water with his purple pectoral fins set wide as wings and the great erect tail slicing through the dark. I wonder how much he sees at that depth, the old man thought. His eye is huge and a horse, with much less eye, can see in the dark. Once I could see quite well in the dark. Not in the absolute dark. But almost as a cat sees.

The sun and his steady movement of his fingers had uncramped his left hand now completely and he began to shift more of the strain to it and he shrugged the muscles of his back to shift the hurt of the cord a little.

'If you're not tired, fish,' he said aloud, 'you must be very strange.'

He felt very tired now and he knew the night would come soon and he tried to think of other things. He thought of the Big Leagues, to him they were the *Gran Ligas*, and he knew that the Yankees of New York were playing the *Tigres* of Detroit.

This is the second day now that I do not know the result of the *juegos*, he thought. But I must have confidence and I must be worthy of the great DiMaggio who does all things perfectly even with the pain of the bone spur in his heel. What is a bone spur? he asked himself. *Un espuela de hueso.* We do not have them. Can it be as painful as the spur of a fighting cock in one's heel? I do not think I could endure that or the loss of the eye and of both eyes and continue to fight as the fighting cocks do. Man is not much beside the great birds and beasts. Still I would rather be that beast down there in the darkness of the sea.

'Unless sharks come,' he said aloud. 'If sharks come, God pity him and me.'

Do you believe the great DiMaggio would stay with a fish as long as I will stay with this one? he thought. I am sure he would and more since he is young and strong. Also his father was a fisherman. But would the bone spur hurt him too much?

'I do not know,' he said aloud. 'I never had a bone spur.'

As the sun set he remembered, to give himself more confidence, the time in the tavern at Casablanca when he had played the hand game with the great negro from Cienfuegos who was the strongest man on the docks. They had gone one day and one night with their elbows on a chalk line on the table and their forearms straight up and their hands gripped tight. Each one was trying to force the other's hand down onto the table. There was much betting and people went in and out of the room under the kerosene lights and he had looked at the arm and hand of the negro and at the negro's face. They changed the referees every four hours after the first eight so that the referees could sleep. Blood came out from under the fingernails of both his and the negro's hands and they looked each other in the eye and at their hands and forearms and the bettors went in and out of the room and sat on high chairs against the wall and watched. The walls were painted bright blue and were of wood and the lamps threw their shadows against them. The negro's shadow was huge and it moved on the wall as the breeze moved the lamps.

The odds would change back and forth all night and they fed the negro rum and lighted cigarettes for him. Then the negro, after the rum, would try for a tremendous effort and once he had the old man, who was not an old man then but was Santiago *El Campeón*, nearly three inches off balance. But the old man had raised his hand up to dead even again. He was sure then that he had the negro, who was a fine man and a great athlete, beaten. And at daylight when the bettors were asking that it be called a draw and the referee was shaking his head, he had unleashed his effort and forced the hand of the negro down and down until it rested on the wood. The match had started on a Sunday morning and ended on a Monday morning. Many of the bettors had asked for a draw because they had to go to work on the docks loading sacks of sugar or at the Havana Coal Company. Otherwise everyone would have wanted it to go to a finish. But he had finished it anyway and before anyone had to go to work.

For a long time after that everyone had called him The Champion and there had been a return match in the spring. But not much money was bet and he had won it quite easily since he had broken the confidence of the negro from Cienfuegos in the first match. After that he had a few matches and then no more. He decided that he could beat anyone if he wanted to badly enough and he decided that it was bad for his right hand for fishing. He had tried a few practice matches with his left hand. But his left hand had always been a traitor and would not do what he called on it to do and he did not trust it.

The sun will bake it out well now, he thought. It should not cramp on me again unless it gets too cold in the night. I wonder what this night will bring.

An aeroplane passed overhead on its course to Miami and he watched its shadow scaring up the schools of flying fish.

'With so much flying fish there should be dolphin,' he said, and leaned back on the line to see if it was possible to gain any on his fish. But he could not and it stayed at the hardness and water-drop shivering that preceded breaking. The boat moved ahead slowly and he watched the aeroplane until he could no longer see it.

It must be very strange in an aeroplane, he thought. I wonder what the sea looks like from that height? They should be able to see the fish well if they do not fly too high. I would like to fly very slowly at two hundred fathoms high and see the fish from above. In the turtle boats I was in the cross-trees of the mast-head and even at that height I saw much. The dolphin look greener from there and you can see their stripes and their purple spots and you can see all of the school as they swim. Why is it that all the fast-moving fish of the dark current have purple backs and usually purple stripes or spots? The dolphin looks green of course because he is really golden. But when he comes to feed, truly hungry, purple stripes show on his sides as on a marlin. Can it be anger, or the greater speed he makes that brings them out?

Just before it was dark, as they passed a great island of Sargasso weed that heaved and swung in the light sea as though the ocean were making love with something under a yellow blanket, his small line was taken by a dolphin. He saw it first when it jumped in the air, true gold in the last of the sun and bending and flapping wildly in the air. It jumped again and again in the acrobatics of its fear and he worked his way back to the stern and crouching and holding the big line with his right hand and arm, he pulled the dolphin in with his left hand, stepping on the gained line each time with his bare left foot. When the fish was at the stern, plunging and cutting from side to side in desperation, the old man leaned over the stern and lifted the burnished gold fish with its purple spots over the stern. Its jaws were working convulsively in quick bites against the hook and it pounded the bottom of the skiff with its long flat body, its tail and its head until he clubbed it across the shining golden head until it shivered and was still.

The old man unhooked the fish, re-baited the line with another sardine and tossed it over. Then he worked his way slowly back to the bow. He washed his left hand and wiped it on his trousers. Then he shifted the heavy line from his right hand to his left and washed his right hand in the sea while he watched the sun go into the ocean and the slant of the big cord.

'He hasn't changed at all,' he said. But watching the movement of the water against his hand he noted that it was perceptibly slower.

'I'll lash the two oars together across the stern and that will slow him in the night,' he said. 'He's good for the night and so am I.'

It would be better to gut the dolphin a little later to save the blood in the meat, he thought. I can do that a little later and lash the oars to make a drag at the same time. I had better keep the fish quiet now and not disturb him too much at sunset. The setting of the sun is a difficult time for all fish.

He let his hand dry in the air then grasped the line with it and eased himself as much as he could and allowed himself to be pulled forward against the wood so that the boat took the strain as much, or more, than he did.

I'm learning how to do it, he thought. This part of it anyway. Then too, remember he hasn't eaten since he took the bait and he is huge and needs much food. I have eaten the whole bonito. Tomorrow I will eat the dolphin. He called it *dorado*. Perhaps I should eat some of it when I clean it. It will be harder to eat than the bonito. But, then, nothing is easy.

'How do you feel, fish?' he asked aloud. 'I feel good and my left hand is better and I have food for a night and a day. Pull the boat, fish.'

He did not truly feel good because the pain from the cord across his back had almost passed pain and gone into a dullness that he mistrusted. But I have had worse things than that, he thought. My hand is only cut a little and the cramp is gone from the other. My legs are all right. Also now I have gained on him in the question of sustenance.

It was dark now as it becomes dark quickly after the sun sets in September. He lay against the worn wood of the bow and rested all that he could. The first stars were out. He did not know the name of Rigel but he saw it and knew soon they would all be out and he would have all his distant friends.

'The fish is my friend too,' he said aloud. 'I have never seen or heard of such a fish. But I must kill him. I am glad we do not have to try to kill the stars.'

Imagine if each day a man must try to kill the moon, he thought. The moon runs away. But imagine if a man each day should have to try to kill the sun? We were born lucky, he thought.

Then he was sorry for the great fish that had nothing to eat and his determination to kill him never relaxed in his sorrow for him. How many people will he feed, he thought. But are they worthy to eat him? No, of course not. There is no one worthy of eating him from the manner of his behavior and his great dignity.

I do not understand these things, he thought. But it is good that we do not have to try to kill the sun or the moon or the stars. It is enough to live on the sea and kill our true brothers.

Now, he thought, I must think about the drag. It has its perils and its merits. I may lose so much line that I will lose him, if he makes his effort and the drag made by the oars is in place and the boat loses all her lightness. Her lightness prolongs both our suffering but it is my safety since he has great speed that he has never yet employed. No matter what passes I must gut the dolphin so he does not spoil and eat some of him to be strong.

Now I will rest an hour more and feel that he is solid and steady before I move back to the stern to do the work and make the decision. In the meantime I can see how he acts and if he shows any changes. The oars are a good trick; but it has reached the time to play for safety! He is much fish still and I saw that the hook was in the corner of his mouth and he has kept his mouth tight shut. The punishment of the hook is nothing. The punishment of hunger, and that he is against something that he does not comprehend, is everything. Rest now, old man, and let him work until your next duty comes.

He rested for what he believed to be two hours. The moon did not rise now until late and he had no way of judging the time. Nor was he really resting except comparatively. He was still bearing the pull of the fish across his shoulders but he placed his left hand on the gunwale of the bow and confided more and more of the resistance to the fish to the skiff itself.

How simple it would be if I could make the line fast, he thought. But with one small lurch he could break it. I must cushion the pull of the line with my body and at all times be ready to give line with both hands.

'But you have not slept yet, old man,' he said aloud. 'It is half a day and a night and now another day and you have not slept. You must devise a way so that you sleep a little if he is quiet and steady. If you do not sleep you might become unclear in the head.'

I'm clear enough in the head, he thought. Too clear. I am as clear as the stars that are my brothers. Still I must sleep. They sleep and the moon and the sun sleep and even the ocean sleeps sometimes on certain days when there is no current and a flat calm.

But remember to sleep, he thought. Make yourself do it and devise some simple and sure way about the lines. Now go back and prepare the dolphin. It is too dangerous to rig the oars as a drag if you must sleep.

I could go without sleeping, he told himself. But it would be too dangerous.

He started to work his way back to the stern on his hands and knees, being careful not to jerk against the fish. He may be half asleep himself, he thought. But I do not want him to rest. He must pull until he dies.

Back in the stern he turned so that his left hand held the strain of the line across his shoulders and drew his knife from its sheath with his right hand. The stars were bright now and he saw the dolphin clearly and he pushed the blade of his knife into his head and drew him out from under the stern. He put one of his feet on the fish and slit him quickly from the vent up to the tip of his lower jaw. Then he put his knife down and gutted him with his right hand, scooping him clean and pulling the gills clear. He felt the maw heavy and slippery in his hands and he slit it open. There were two flying fish inside. They were fresh and hard and he laid them side by side and dropped the guts and the gills over the stern. They sank leaving a trail of phosphorescence in the water. The dolphin was cold and a leprous gray-white now in the starlight and the old man skinned one side of him while he held his right foot on the fish's head. Then he turned him over and skinned the other side and cut each side off from the head down to the tail.

He slid the carcass overboard and looked to see if there was any swirl in the water. But there was only the light of its slow descent. He turned then and placed the two flying fish inside the two fillets of fish and putting his knife back in its sheath, he worked his way slowly back to the bow. His back was bent with the weight of the line across it and he carried the fish in his right hand.

Back in the bow he laid the two fillets of fish out on the wood with the flying fish beside them. After that he settled the line across his shoulders in a new place and held it again with his left hand resting on the gunwale. Then he leaned over the side and washed the flying fish in the water, noting the speed of the water against his hand. His hand was phosphorescent from skinning the fish and he watched the flow of the water against it. The flow was less strong and as he rubbed the side of his hand against the planking of the skiff, particles of phosphorus floated off and drifted slowly astern.

'He is tiring or he is resting,' the old man said. 'Now let me get through the eating of this dolphin and get some rest and a little sleep.'

Under the stars and with the night colder all the time he ate half of one of the dolphin fillets and one of the flying fish, gutted and with its head cut off.

'What an excellent fish dolphin is to eat cooked,' he said. 'And what a miserable fish raw. I will never go in a boat again without salt or limes.'

If I had brains I would have splashed water on the bow all day and drying, it would have made salt, he thought. But then I did not hook the dolphin until almost sunset. Still it was a lack of preparation. But I have chewed it all well and I am not nauseated.

The sky was clouding over to the east and one after another the stars he knew were gone. It looked now as though he were moving into a great canyon of clouds and the wind had dropped.

'There will be bad weather in three or four days,' he said. 'But not tonight and not tomorrow. Rig now to get some sleep, old man, while the fish is calm and steady.'

He held the line tight in his right hand and then pushed his thigh against his right hand as he leaned all his weight against the wood of the bow. Then he passed the line a little lower on his shoulders and braced his left hand on it.

My right hand can hold it as long as it is braced, he thought. If it relaxes in sleep my left hand will wake me as the line goes out. It is hard on the right hand. But he is used to punishment. Even if I sleep twenty minutes or a half an hour it is good. He lay forward cramping himself against the line with all of his body, putting all his weight onto his right band, and he was asleep.

He did not dream of the lions but instead of a vast school of porpoises that stretched for eight or ten miles and it was in the time of their mating and they would leap high into the air and return into the same hole they had made in the water when they leaped.

Then he dreamed that he was in the village on his bed and there was a norther and he was very cold and his right arm was asleep because his head had rested on it instead of a pillow.

After that he began to dream of the long yellow beach and he saw the first of the lions come down onto it in the early dark and then the other lions came and he rested his chin on the wood of the bows where the ship lay anchored with the evening off-shore breeze and he waited to see if there would be more lions and he was happy.

The moon had been up for a long time but he slept on and the fish pulled on steadily and the boat moved into the tunnel of clouds.

He woke with the jerk of his right fist coming up against his face and the line burning out through his right hand. He had no feeling of his left hand but he braked all he could with his right and the line rushed out. Finally his left hand found the line and he leaned back against the line and now it burned his back and his left hand, and his left hand was taking all the strain and cutting badly. He looked back at the coils of line and they were feeding smoothly. Just then the fish jumped making a great bursting of the ocean and then a heavy fall. Then he jumped again and again and the boat was going fast although line was still racing out and the old man was raising the strain to breaking point and raising it to breaking point again and again. He had been pulled down tight onto the bow and his face was in the cut slice of dolphin and he could not move.

This is what we waited for, he thought. So now let us take it.

Make him pay for the line, he thought. Make him pay for it.

He could not see the fish's jumps but only heard the breaking of the ocean and the heavy splash as he fell. The speed of the line was cutting his hands badly but he had always known this would happen and he tried to keep the cutting across the calloused parts and not let the line slip into the palm nor cut the fingers.

If the boy was here he would wet the coils of line, he thought. Yes. If the boy were here. If the boy were here.

The line went out and out and out but it was slowing now and he was making the fish earn each inch of it. Now he got his head up from the wood and out of the slice of fish that his cheek had crushed. Then he was on his knees and then he rose slowly to his feet. He was ceding line but more slowly all the time. He worked back to where he could feel with his foot the coils of line that he could not see. There was plenty of line still and now the fish had to pull the friction of all that new line through the water.

Yes, he thought. And now he has jumped more than a dozen times and filled the sacs along his back with air and he cannot go down deep to die where I cannot bring him up. He will start circling soon and then I must work on him. I wonder what started him so suddenly? Could it have been hunger that made him desperate, or was he frightened by something in the night? Maybe he suddenly felt fear. But he was such a calm, strong fish and he seemed so fearless and so confident. It is strange.

'You better be fearless and confident yourself, old man,' he said. 'You're holding him again but you cannot get line. But soon he has to circle.'

The old man held him with his left hand and his shoulders now and stooped down and scooped up water in his right hand to get the crushed dolphin flesh off of his face. He was afraid that it might nauseate him and he would vomit and lose his strength. When his face was cleaned he washed his right hand in the water over the side and then let it stay in the salt water while he watched the first light come before the sunrise. He's headed almost east, he thought. That means he is tired and going with the current. Soon he will have to circle. Then our true work begins.

After he judged that his right hand had been in the water long enough he took it out and looked at it.

'It is not bad,' he said. 'And pain does not matter to a man.'

He took hold of the line carefully so that it did not fit into any of the fresh line cuts and shifted his weight so that he could put his left hand into the sea on the other side of the skiff.

'You did not do so badly for something worthless,' he said to his left hand. 'But there was a moment when I could not find you.'

Why was I not born with two good hands? he thought. Perhaps it was my fault in not training that one properly. But God knows he has had enough chances to learn. He did not do so badly in the night, though, and he has only cramped once. If he cramps again let the line cut him off.

When he thought that he knew that he was not being clear-headed and he thought he should chew some more of the dolphin. But I can't, he told himself. It is better to be light-headed than to lose your strength from nausea. And I know I cannot keep it if I eat it since my face was in it. I will keep it for an emergency until it goes bad. But it is too late to try for strength now through nourishment. You're stupid, he told himself. Eat the other flying fish.

It was there, cleaned and ready, and he picked it up with his left hand and ate it chewing the bones carefully and eating all of it down to the tail.

It has more nourishment than almost any fish, he thought. At least the kind of strength that I need. Now I have done what I can, he thought. Let him begin to circle and let the fight come.

The sun was rising for the third time since he had put to sea when the fish started to circle.

He could not see by the slant of the line that the fish was circling. It was too early for that. He just felt a faint slackening of the pressure of the line and he commenced to pull on it gently with his right hand. It tightened, as always, but just when he reached the point where it would break, line began to come in. He slipped his shoulders and head from under the line and began to pull in line steadily and gently. He used both of his hands in a swinging motion and tried to do the pulling as much as he could with his body and his legs. His old legs and shoulders pivoted with the swinging of the pulling.

'It is a very big circle,' he said. 'But he is circling.'

Then the line would not come in any more and he held it until he saw the drops jumping from it in the sun. Then it started out

and the old man knelt down and let it go grudgingly back into the dark water.

'He is making the far part of his circle now,' he said. I must hold all I can, he thought. The strain will shorten his circle each time. Perhaps in an hour I will see him. Now I must convince him and then I must kill him.

But the fish kept on circling slowly and the old man was wet with sweat and tired deep into his bones two hours later. But the circles were much shorter now and from the way the line slanted he could tell the fish had risen steadily while he swam.

For an hour the old man had been seeing black spots before his eyes and the sweat salted his eyes and salted the cut over his eye and on his forehead. He was not afraid of the black spots. They were normal at the tension that he was pulling on the line. Twice, though, he had felt faint and dizzy and that had worried him.

'I could not fail myself and die on a fish like this,' he said. 'Now that I have him coming so beautifully, God help me endure. I'll say a hundred Our Fathers and a hundred Hail Marys. But I cannot say them now.'

Consider them said, he thought. I'll say them later.

Just then he felt a sudden banging and jerking on the line he held with his two hands. It was sharp and hard-feeling and heavy.

He is hitting the wire leader with his spear, he thought. That was bound to come. He had to do that. It may make him jump though and I would rather he stayed circling now. The jumps were necessary for him to take air. But after that each one can widen the opening of the hook wound and he can throw the hook.

'Don't jump, fish,' he said. 'Don't jump.'

The fish hit the wire several times more and each time he shook his head the old man gave up a little line.

I must hold his pain where it is, he thought. Mine does not matter. I can control mine. But his pain could drive him mad.

After a while the fish stopped beating at the wire and started circling slowly again. The old man was gaining line steadily now. But he felt faint again. He lifted some sea water with his left hand and put it on his head. Then he put more on and rubbed the back of his neck.

'I have no cramps,' he said. 'He'll be up soon and I can last. You have to last. Don't even speak of it.'

He kneeled against the bow and, for a moment, slipped the line over his back again. I'll rest now while he goes out on the circle and then stand up and work on him when he comes in, he decided.

It was a great temptation to rest in the bow and let the fish make one circle by himself without recovering any line. But when the strain showed the fish had turned to come toward the boat, the old man rose to his feet and started the pivoting and the weaving pulling that brought in all the line he gained.

I'm tireder than I have ever been, he thought, and now the trade wind is rising. But that will be good to take him in with. I need that badly.

'I'll rest on the next turn as he goes out,' he said. 'I feel much better. Then in two or three turns more I will have him.'

His straw hat was far on the back of his head and he sank down into the bow with the pull of the line as he felt the fish turn.

You work now, fish, he thought. I'll take you at the turn.

The sea had risen considerably. But it was a fair-weather breeze and he had to have it to get home.

'I'll just steer south and west,' he said. 'A man is never lost at sea and it is a long island.'

It was on the third turn that he saw the fish first.

He saw him first as a dark shadow that took so long to pass under the boat that he could not believe its length.

'No,' he said. 'He can't be that big.'

But he was that big and at the end of this circle he came to the surface only thirty yards away and the man saw his tail out of water. It was higher than a big scythe blade and a very pale lavender above the dark blue water. It raked back and as the fish swam just below the surface the old man could see his huge bulk and the purple stripes that banded him. His dorsal fin was down and his huge pectorals were spread wide.

On this circle the old man could see the fish's eye and the two gray sucking fish that swain around him. Sometimes they attached themselves to him. Sometimes they darted off. Sometimes they would swim easily in his shadow. They were each over three feet long and when they swam fast they lashed their whole bodies like eels.

The old man was sweating now but from something else besides the sun. On each calm placid turn the fish made he was gaining line and he was sure that in two turns more he would have a chance to get the harpoon in.

But I must get him close, close, close, he thought. I mustn't try for the head. I must get the heart.

'Be calm and strong, old man,' he said.

On the next circle the fish's back was out but he was a little too far from the boat. On the next circle he was still too far away but he was higher out of water and the old man was sure that by gaining some more line he could have him alongside.

He had rigged his harpoon long before and its coil of light rope was in a round basket and the end was made fast to the bitt in the bow.

The fish was coming in on his circle now calm and beautiful looking and only his great tail moving. The old man pulled on him all that he could to bring him closer. For just a moment the fish turned a little on his side. Then he straightened himself and began another circle.

'I moved him,' the old man said. 'I moved him then.'

He felt faint again now but he held on the great fish all the strain that he could. I moved him, he thought. Maybe this time I can get him over. Pull, hands, he thought. Hold up, legs. Last for me, head. Last for me. You never went. This time I'll pull him over.

But when he put all of his effort on, starting it well out before the fish came alongside and pulling with all his strength, the fish pulled part way over and then righted himself and swam away.

'Fish,' the old man said. 'Fish, you are going to have to die anyway. Do you have to kill me too?'

That way nothing is accomplished, he thought. His mouth was too dry to speak but he could not reach for the water now. I must get him alongside this time, he thought. I am not good for many more turns. Yes you are, he told himself. You're good for ever.

On the next turn, he nearly had him. But again the fish righted himself and swam slowly away.

You are killing me, fish, the old man thought. But you have a right to. Never have I seen a greater, or more beautiful, or a calmer or more noble thing than you, brother. Come on and kill me. I do not care who kills who.

Now you are getting confused in the head, he thought. You must keep your head clear. Keep your head clear and know how to suffer like a man. Or a fish, he thought.

'Clear up, head,' he said in a voice he could hardly hear. 'Clear up.'

Twice more it was the same on the turns.

I do not know, the old man thought. He had been on the point of feeling himself go each time. I do not know. But I will try it once more.

He tried it once more and he felt himself going when he turned the fish. The fish righted himself and swam off again slowly with the great tail weaving in the air.

I'll try it again, the old man promised, although his hands were mushy now and he could only see well in flashes.

He tried it again and it was the same. So, he thought, and he felt himself going before he started; I will try it once again.

He took all his pain and what was left of his strength and his long gone pride and he put it against the fish's agony and the fish came over onto his side and swam gently on his side, his bill almost touching the planking of the skiff and started to pass the boat, long, deep, wide, silver and barred with purple and interminable in the water.

The old man dropped the line and put his foot on it and lifted the harpoon as high as he could and drove it down with all his strength, and more strength he had just summoned, into the fish's side just behind the great chest fin that rose high in the air to the altitude of the man's chest. He felt the iron go in and he leaned on it and drove it further and then pushed all his weight after it.

Then the fish came alive, with his death in him, and rose high out of the water showing all his great length and width and all his power and his beauty. He seemed to hang in the air above the old man in the skiff. Then he fell into the water with a crash that sent spray over the old man and over all of the skiff.

The old man felt faint and sick and he could not see well. But he cleared the harpoon line and let it run slowly through his raw hands and, when he could see, he saw the fish was on his back with his silver belly up. The shaft of the harpoon was projecting at an angle from the fish's shoulder and the sea was discolouring with the red of the blood from his heart. First it was dark as a shoal in the blue water that was more than a mile deep. Then it spread like a cloud. The fish was silvery and still and floated with the waves.

The old man looked carefully in the glimpse of vision that he had. Then he took two turns of the harpoon line around the bitt in the bow and laid his head on his hands.

'Keep my head dear,' he said against the wood of the bow. 'I am a tired old man. But I have killed this fish which is my brother and now I must do the slave work.'

Now I must prepare the nooses and the rope to lash him alongside, he thought. Even if we were two and swamped her to load him and bailed her out, this skiff would never hold him. I must prepare everything, then bring him in and lash him well and step the mast and set sail for home.

He started to pull the fish in to have him alongside so that he could pass a line through his gills and out his mouth and make his head fast alongside the bow. I want to see him, he thought, and to touch and to feel him. He is my fortune, he thought. But that is not why I wish to feel him. I think I felt his heart, he thought. When I pushed on the harpoon shaft the second time. Bring him in now and make him fast and get the noose around his tail and another around his middle to bind him to the skiff.

'Get to work, old man,' he said. He took a very small drink of the water. 'There is very much slave work to be done now that the fight is over.'

He looked up at the sky and then out to his fish. He looked at the sun carefully. It is not much more than noon, he thought. And the trade wind is rising. The lines all mean nothing now. The boy and I will splice them when we are home.

'Come on, fish,' he said. But the fish did not come. Instead he lay there wallowing now in the seas and the old man pulled the skiff upon to him.

When he was even with him and had the fish's head against the bow he could not believe his size. But he untied the harpoon rope from the bitt, passed it through the fish's gills and out his jaws, made a turn around his sword then passed the rope through the other gill, made another turn around the bill and knotted the double rope and made it fast to the bitt in the bow. He cut the rope then and went astern to noose the tail. The fish had turned silver from his original purple and silver, and the stripes showed the same pale violet colour as his tail. They were wider than a man's hand with his fingers spread and the fish's eye looked as detached as the mirrors in a periscope or as a saint in a procession.

'It was the only way to kill him,' the old man said. He was feeling better since the water and he knew he would not go away and his head was clear. He's over fifteen hundred pounds the way he is, he thought. Maybe much more. If he dresses out two-thirds of that at thirty cents a pound?

'I need a pencil for that,' he said. 'My head is not that clear. But I think the great DiMaggio would be proud of me today. I had no bone spurs. But the hands and the back hurt truly.' I wonder what a bone spur is, he thought. Maybe we have them without knowing of it.

He made the fish fast to bow and stern and to the middle thwart. He was so big it was like lashing a much bigger skiff alongside. He cut a piece of line and tied the fish's lower jaw against his bill so his mouth would not open and they would sail as cleanly as possible. Then he stepped the mast and, with the stick that was his gaff and with his boom rigged, the patched sail drew, the boat began to move, and half lying in the stern he sailed south-west.

He did not need a compass to tell him where south-west was. He only needed the feel of the trade wind and the drawing of the sail. I better put a small line out with a spoon on it and try and get something to eat and drink for the moisture. But he could not find a spoon and his sardines were rotten. So he hooked a patch of yellow Gulf weed with the gaff as they passed and shook it so that the small shrimps that were in it fell onto the planking of the skiff. There were more than a dozen of them and they jumped and kicked like sand fleas. The old man pinched their heads off with his thumb and forefinger and ate them chewing up the shells and the tails. They were very tiny but he knew they were nourishing and they tasted good.

The old man still had two drinks of water in the bottle and he used half of one after he had eaten the shrimps. The skiff was sailing well considering the handicaps and he steered with the tiller under his arm. He could see the fish and he had only to look at his hands and feel his back against the stern to know that this had truly happened and was not a dream. At one time when he was feeling so badly toward the end, he had thought perhaps it was a dream. Then when he had seen the fish come out of the water and hang motionless in the sky before he fell, he was sure there was some great strangeness and he could not believe it. Then he could not see well, although now he saw as well as ever.

Now he knew there was the fish and his hands and back were no dream. The hands cure quickly, he thought. I bled them clean and the salt water will heal them. The dark water of the true gulf is the greatest healer that there is. All I must do is keep the head clear. The hands have done their work and we sail well. With his mouth shut and his tail straight up and down we sail like brothers. Then his head started to become a little unclear and he thought, is he bringing me in or am I bringing him in? If I were towing him behind there would be no question. Nor if the fish were in the skiff, with all dignity gone, there would be no question either. But they were sailing together lashed side by side and the old man thought, let him bring me in if it pleases him. I am only better than him through trickery and he meant me no harm.

They sailed well and the old man soaked his hands in the salt water and tried to keep his head clear. There were high cumulus clouds and enough cirrus above them so that the old man knew the breeze would last all night. The old man looked at the fish constantly to make sure it was true. It was an hour before the first shark hit him.

The shark was not an accident. He had come up from deep down in the water as the dark cloud of blood had settled and dispersed in the mile-deep sea. He had come up so fast and absolutely without caution that he broke the surface of the blue water and was in the sun. Then he fell back into the sea and picked up the scent and started swimming on the course the skiff and the fish had taken.

Sometimes he lost the scent. But he would pick it up again, or have just a trace of it, and he swam fast and hard on the course. He was a very big Mako shark built to swim as fast as the fastest fish in the sea and everything about him was beautiful except his jaws. His back was as blue as a swordfish's and his belly was silver and his hide was smooth and handsome. He was built as a swordfish except for his huge jaws which were tight shut now as he swam fast, just under the surface with his high dorsal fin knifing through the water without wavering. Inside the closed double lip of his jaws all of his eight rows of teeth were slanted inwards. They were not the ordinary pyramid-shaped teeth of most sharks. They were shaped like a man's fingers when they are crisped like claws. They were nearly as long as the fingers of the old man and they had razor-sharp cutting edges on both sides. This was a fish built to feed on all the fishes in the sea, that were so fast and strong and well armed that they had no other enemy. Now he speeded up as he smelled the fresher scent and his blue dorsal fin cut the water.

When the old man saw him coming he knew that this was a shark that had no fear at all and would do exactly what he wished. He prepared the harpoon and made the rope fast while he watched the shark come on. The rope was short as it lacked what he had cut away to lash the fish.

The old man's head was clear and good now and he was full of resolution but he had little hope. It was too good to last, he thought. He took one look at the great fish as he watched the shark close in. It might as well have been a dream, he thought. I cannot keep him from hitting me but maybe I can get him. *Dentuso*, he thought. Bad luck to your mother.

The shark closed fast astern and when he hit the fish the old man saw his mouth open and his strange eyes and the clicking chop of the teeth as he drove forward in the meat just above the tail. The shark's head was out of water and his back was coming out and the old man could hear the noise of skin and flesh ripping on the big fish when he rammed the harpoon down onto the shark's head at a spot where the line between his eyes intersected with the line that ran straight back from his nose. There were no such lines. There was only the heavy sharp blue head and the big eyes and the clicking, thrusting all-swallowing jaws. But that was the location of the brain and the old man hit it. He hit it with his blood mushed hands driving a good harpoon with all his strength. He hit it without hope but with resolution and complete malignancy.

The shark swung over and the old man saw his eye was not alive and then he swung over once again, wrapping himself in two loops of the rope. The old man knew that he was dead but the shark would not accept it. Then, on his back, with his tail lashing and his jaws clicking, the shark ploughed over the water as a speedboat does. The water was white where his tail beat it and three-quarters of his body was clear above the water when the rope came taut, shivered, and then snapped. The shark lay quietly for a little while on the surface and the old man watched him. Then he went down very slowly.

'He took about forty pounds,' the old man said aloud. He took my harpoon too and all the rope, he thought, and now my fish bleeds again and there will be others.

He did not like to look at the fish any more since he had been mutilated. When the fish had been hit it was as though he himself were hit.

But I killed the shark that hit my fish, he thought. And he was the biggest *dentuso* that I have ever seen. And God knows that I have seen big ones.

It was too good to last, he thought. I wish it had been a dream now and that I had never hooked the fish and was alone in bed on the newspapers.

'But man is not made for defeat,' he said. 'A man can be destroyed but not defeated.' I am sorry that I killed the fish though, he thought. Now the bad time is coming and I do not even have the harpoon. The *dentuso* is cruel and able and strong and intelligent. But I was more intelligent than he was. Perhaps not, he thought. Perhaps I was only better armed.

'Don't think, old man,' he said aloud. 'Sail on this course and take it when it comes.

But I must think, he thought. Because it is all I have left. That and baseball. I wonder how the great DiMaggio would have liked the way I hit him in the brain? It was no great thing, he thought. Any man could do it. But do you think my hands were as great a handicap as the bone spurs? I cannot know. I never had anything wrong with my heel except the time the sting ray stung it when I stepped on him when swimming and paralyzed the lower leg and made the unbearable pain.

'Think about something cheerful, old man,' he said. 'Every minute now you are closer to home. You sail lighter for the loss of forty pounds.'

He knew quite well the pattern of what could happen when he reached the inner part of the current. But there was nothing to be done now.

'Yes there is,' he said aloud. 'I can lash my knife to the butt of one of the oars.'

So he did that with the tiller under his arm and the sheet of the sail under his foot.

'Now,' he said. 'I am still an old man. But I am not unarmed.'

The breeze was fresh now and he sailed on well. He watched only the forward part of the fish and some of his hope returned.

It is silly not to hope, he thought. Besides I believe it is a sin. Do not think about sin, he thought. There are enough problems now without sin. Also I have no understanding of it.

I have no understanding of it and I am not sure that I believe in it. Perhaps it was a sin to kill the fish. I suppose it was even though I did it to keep me alive and feed many people. But then everything is a sin. Do not think about sin. It is much too late for that and there are people who are paid to do it. Let them think about it. You were born to be a fisherman as the fish was born to be a fish. San Pedro was a fisherman as was the father of the great DiMaggio.

But he liked to think about all things that he was involved in and since there was nothing to read and he did not have a radio, he thought much and he kept on thinking about sin. You did not kill the fish only to keep alive and to sell for food, he thought. You killed him for pride and because you are a fisherman. You loved him when he was alive and you loved him after. If you love him, it is not a sin to kill him. Or is it more?

'You think too much, old man,' he said aloud.

But you enjoyed killing the *dentuso*, he thought. He lives on the live fish as you do. He is not a scavenger nor just a moving appetite as some sharks are. He is beautiful and noble and knows no fear of anything.

'I killed him in self-defense,' the old man said aloud. 'And I killed him well.'

Besides, he thought, everything kills everything else in some way. Fishing kills me exactly as it keeps me alive. The boy keeps me alive, he thought. I must not deceive myself too much.

He leaned over the side and pulled loose a piece of the meat of the fish where the shark had cut him. He chewed it and noted its quality and its good taste. It was firm and juicy, like meat, but it was not red. There was no stringiness in it and he knew that it would bring the highest price in the market. But there was no way to keep its scent out of the water and the old man knew that a very had time was coming.

The breeze was steady. It had backed a little further into the north-east and he knew that meant that it would not fall off. The old man looked ahead of him but he could see no sails nor could he see the hull nor the smoke of any ship. There were only the flying fish that went up from his bow sailing away to either side and the yellow patches of Gulf weed. He could not even see a bird.

He had sailed for two hours, resting in the stern and sometimes chewing a bit of the meat from the marlin, trying to rest and to be strong, when he saw the first of the two sharks.

'Ay,' he said aloud. There is no translation for this word and perhaps it is just a noise such as a man might make, involuntarily, feeling the nail go through his hands and into the wood.

'Galanos,' he said aloud. He had seen the second fin now coming up behind the first and had identified them as shovel-nosed sharks by the brown, triangular fin and the sweeping movements of the tail. They had the scent and were excited and in the stupidity of their great hunger they were losing and finding the scent in their excitement. But they were closing all the time.

The old man made the sheet fast and jammed the tiller. Then he took up the oar with the knife lashed to it. He lifted it as lightly as he could because his hands rebelled at the pain. Then he opened and closed them on it lightly to loosen them. He closed them firmly so they would take the pain now and would not flinch and watched the sharks come. He could see their wide, flattened, shovel-pointed heads now and their white-tipped wide pectoral fins. They were hateful sharks, bad smelling, scavengers as well as killers, and when they were hungry they would bite at an oar or the rudder of a boat. It was these sharks that would cut the turtles' legs and flippers off when the turtles were asleep on the surface, and they would hit a man in the water, if they were hungry, even if the man had no smell of fish blood nor of fish slime on him.

'Ay,' the old man said. '*Galanos*. Come on *galanos*.'

They came. But they did not come as the Mako had come. One turned and went out of sight under the skiff and the old man could feel the skiff shake as he jerked and pulled on the fish. The other watched the old man with his slitted yellow eyes and then came in fast with his half circle of jaws wide to hit the fish where he had already been bitten. The line showed clearly on the top of his brown head and back where the brain joined the spinal cord and the old man drove the knife on the oar into the juncture, withdrew it, and drove it in again into the shark's yellow cat-like eyes. The shark let go of the fish and slid down, swallowing what he had taken as he died.

The skiff was still shaking with the destruction the other shark was doing to the fish and the old man let go the sheet so that the skiff would swing broadside and bring the shark out from under.

When he saw the shark he leaned over the side and punched at him. He hit only meat and the hide was set hard and he barely got the knife in. The blow hurt not only his hands but his shoulder too. But the shark came up fast with his head out and the old man hit him squarely in the center of his flat-topped head as his nose came out of water and lay against the fish. The old man withdrew the blade and punched the shark exactly in the same spot again. He still hung to the fish with his jaws hooked and the old man stabbed him in his left eye. The shark still hung there.

'No?' the old man said and he drove the blade between the vertebrae and the brain. It was an easy shot now and he felt the cartilage sever. The old man reversed the oar and put the blade between the shark's jaws to open them. He twisted the blade and as the shark slid loose he said, 'Go on, *galano*. Slide down a mile deep. Go see your friend, or maybe it's your mother.'

The old man wiped the blade of his knife and laid down the oar. Then he found the sheet and the sail filled and he brought the skiff on to her course.

'They must have taken a quarter of him and of the best meat,' he said aloud. 'I wish it were a dream and that I had never hooked him. I'm sorry about it, fish. It makes everything wrong.' He stopped and he did not want to look at the fish now. Drained of blood and awash he looked the colour of the silver backing of a minor and his stripes still showed.

'I shouldn't have gone out so far, fish,' he said. 'Neither for you nor for me. I'm sorry, fish.'

Now, he said to himself. Look to the lashing on the knife and see if it has been cut. Then get your hand in order because there still is more to come.

'I wish I had a stone for the knife,' the old man said after he had checked the lashing on the oar butt. 'I should have brought a stone.' You should have brought many things, he thought. But you did not bring them, old man. Now is no time to think of what you do not have. Think of what you can do with what there is.

'You give me much good counsel,' he said aloud. 'I'm tired of it.'

He held the tiller under his arm and soaked both his hands in the water as the skiff drove forward.

'God knows how much that last one took,' he said. 'But she's much lighter now.' He did not want to think of the mutilated under-side of the fish. He knew that each of the jerking bumps of the shark had been meat torn away and that the fish now made a trail for all sharks as wide as a highway through the sea.

He was a fish to keep a man all winter, he thought. Don't think of that. Just rest and try to get your hands in shape to defend what is left of him. The blood smell from my hands means nothing now with all that scent in the water. Besides they do not bleed much. There is nothing cut that means anything. The bleeding may keep the left from cramping.

What can I think of now? he thought. Nothing. I must think of nothing and wait for the next ones. I wish it had really been a dream, he thought. But who knows? It might have turned out well.

The next shark that came was a single shovelnose. He came like a pig to the trough if a pig had a mouth so wide that you could put your head in it. The old man let him hit the fish and then drove the knife on the oar down into his brain. But the shark jerked backwards as he rolled and the knife blade snapped.

The old man settled himself to steer. He did not even watch

the big shark sinking slowly in the water, showing first life-size, then small, then tiny. That always fascinated the old man. But he did not even watch it now.

'I have the gaff now,' he said. 'But it will do no good. I have the two oars and the tiller and the short club.'

Now they have beaten me, he thought. I am too old to club sharks to death. But I will try it as long as I have the oars and the short club and the tiller.

He put his hands in the water again to soak them. It was getting late in the afternoon and he saw nothing but the sea and the sky. There was more wind in the sky than there had been, and soon he hoped that he would see land.

'You're tired, old man,' he said. 'You're tired inside.'

The sharks did not hit him again until just before sunset.

The old man saw the brown fins coming along the wide trail the fish must make in the water. They were not even quartering on the scent. They were headed straight for the skiff swimming side by side.

He jammed the tiller, made the sheet fast and reached under the stern for the club. It was an oar handle from a broken oar sawed off to about two and a half feet in length. He could only use it effectively with one hand because of the grip of the handle and he took good hold of it with his right hand, flexing his hand on it, as he watched the sharks come. They were both *galanos*.

I must let the first one get a good hold and hit him on the point of the nose or straight across the top of the head, he thought.

The two sharks closed together and as he saw the one nearest him open his jaws and sink them into the silver side of the fish, he raised the club high and brought it down heavy and slamming onto the top of the shark's broad head. He felt the rubbery solidity as the club came down. But he felt the rigidity of bone too and he struck the shark once more hard across the point of the nose as he slid down from the fish.

The other shark had been in and out and now came in again with his jaws wide. The old man could see pieces of the meat of the fish spilling white from the corner of his jaws as he bumped the fish and closed his jaws. He swung at him and hit only the head and the shark looked at him and wrenched the meat loose. The old man swung the club down on him again as he slipped away to swallow and hit only the heavy solid rubberiness.

'Come on, *galano*,' the old man said. 'Come in again.'

The shark came in in a rush and the old man hit him as he shut his jaws. He hit him solidly and from as high up as he could raise the club. This time he felt the bone at the base of the brain and he hit him again in the same place while the shark tore the meat loose sluggishly and slid down from the fish.

The old man watched for him to come again but neither shark showed. Then he saw one on the surface swimming in circles. He did not see the fin of the other.

I could not expect to kill them, he thought. I could have in my time. But I have hurt them both badly and neither one can feel very good. If I could have used a bat with two hands I could have killed the first one surely. Even now, he thought.

He did not want to look at the fish. He knew that half of him had been destroyed. The sun had gone down while he had been in the fight with the sharks.

'It will be dark soon,' he said. 'Then I should see the glow of Havana. If I am too far to the eastward I will see the lights of one of the new beaches.'

I cannot be too far out now, he thought. I hope no one has been too worried. There is only the boy to worry, of course. But I am sure he would have confidence. Many of the older fishermen will worry. Many others too, he thought. I live in a good town.

He could not talk to the fish any more because the fish had been ruined too badly. Then something came into his head.

'Half-fish,' he said. 'Fish that you were. I am sorry that I went too far out. I ruined us both. But we have killed many sharks, you and I, and ruined many others. How many did you ever kill, old fish? You do not have that spear on your head for nothing.'

He liked to think of the fish and what he could do to a shark if he were swimming free. I should have chopped the bill off to fight them with, he thought. But there was no hatchet and then there was no knife.

But if I had, and could have lashed it to an oar butt, what a weapon. Then we might have fought them together. What will you do now if they come in the night? What can you do?

'Fight them,' he said. 'I'll fight them until I die.'

But in the dark now and no glow showing and no lights and only the wind and the steady pull of the sail he felt that perhaps he was already dead. He put his two hands together and felt the palms. They were not dead and he could bring the pain of life by simply opening and closing them. He leaned his back against the stern and knew he was not dead. His shoulders told him.

I have all those prayers I promised if I caught the fish, he thought. But I am too tired to say them now. I better get the sack and put it over my shoulders.

He lay in the stern and steered and watched for the glow to come in the sky. I have half of him, he thought. Maybe I'll have the luck to bring the forward half in. I should have some luck. No, he said. You violated your luck when you went too far outside.

'Don't be silly,' he said aloud. 'And keep awake and steer. You may have much luck yet.'

'I'd like to buy some if there's any place they sell it,' he said.

What could I buy it with? he asked himself. Could I buy it with a lost harpoon and a broken knife and two bad hands?

'You might,' he said. 'You tried to buy it with eighty-four days at sea. They nearly sold it to you too.'

I must not think nonsense, he thought. Luck is a thing that comes in many forms and who can recognize her? I would take some though in any form and pay what they asked. I wish I could see the glow from the lights, he thought. I wish too many things. But that is the thing I wish for now. He tried to settle more comfortably to steer and from his pain he knew he was not dead.

He saw the reflected glare of the lights of the city at what must have been around ten o'clock at night. They were only perceptible at first as the light is in the sky before the moon rises. Then they were steady to see across the ocean which was rough now with the increasing breeze. He steered inside of the glow and he thought that now, soon, he must hit the edge of the stream.

Now it is over, he thought. They will probably hit me again. But what can a man do against them in the dark without a weapon?

He was stiff and sore now and his wounds and all of the strained parts of his body hurt with the cold of the night. I hope I do not have to fight again, he thought. I hope so much I do not have to fight again.

But by midnight he fought and this time he knew the fight was useless. They came in a pack and he could only see the lines in the water that their fins made and their phosphorescence as they threw themselves on the fish. He clubbed at heads and heard the jaws chop and the shaking of the skiff as they took hold below. He clubbed desperately at what he could only feel and hear and he felt something seize the club and it was gone.

He jerked the tiller free from the rudder and beat and chopped with it, holding it in both hands and driving it down again and again. But they were up to the bow now and driving in one after the other and together, tearing off the pieces of meat that showed glowing below the sea as they turned to come once more.

One came, finally, against the head itself and he knew that it was over. He swung the tiller across the shark's head where the jaws were caught in the heaviness of the fish's head which would not tear. He swung it once and twice and again. He heard the tiller break and he lunged at the shark with the splintered butt. He felt it go in and knowing it was sharp he drove it in again. The shark let go and rolled away. That was the last shark of the pack that came. There was nothing more for them to eat.

The old man could hardly breathe now and he felt a strange taste in his mouth. It was coppery and sweet and he was afraid of it for a moment. But there was not much of it.

He spat into the ocean and said, 'Eat that, *galanos*. And make a dream you've killed a man.'

He knew he was beaten now finally and without remedy and he went back to the stern and found the jagged end of the tiller would fit in the slot of the rudder well enough for him to steer. He settled the sack around his shoulders and put the skiff on her course. He sailed lightly now and he had no thoughts nor any feelings of any kind. He was past everything now and he sailed the skiff to make his home port as well and as intelligently as he could. In the night sharks hit the carcass as someone might pick up crumbs from the table. The old man paid no attention to them and did not pay any attention to anything except steering. He only noticed how lightly and how well the skiff sailed now there was no great weight beside her.

She's good, he thought. She is sound and not harmed in any way except for the tiller. That is easily replaced.

He could feel he was inside the current now and he could see the lights of the beach colonies along the shore. He knew where he was now and it was nothing to get home.

The wind is our friend, anyway, he thought. Then he added, sometimes. And the great sea with our friends and our enemies. And bed, he thought. Bed is my friend. Just bed, he thought. Bed will be a great thing. It is easy when you are beaten, he thought. I never knew how easy it was. And what beat you, he thought.

'Nothing,' he said aloud. 'I went out too far.'

When he sailed into the little harbour the lights of the Terrace were out and he knew everyone was in bed. The breeze had risen steadily and was blowing strongly now. It was quiet in the harbour though and he sailed up onto the little patch of shingle below the rocks. There was no one to help him so he pulled the boat up as far as he could. Then he stepped out and made her fast to a rock.

He unstepped the mast and furled the sail and tied it. Then he shouldered the mast and started to climb. It was then he knew the depth of his tiredness. He stopped for a moment and looked back and saw in the reflection from the street light the great tail of the fish standing up well behind the skiff's stern. He saw the white naked line of his backbone and the dark mass of the head with the projecting bill and all the nakedness between.

He started to climb again and at the top he fell and lay for some time with the mast across his shoulder. He tried to get up. But it was too difficult and he sat there with the mast on his shoulder and looked at the road. A cat passed on the far side going about its business and the old man watched it. Then he just watched the road.

Finally he put the mast down and stood up. He picked the mast up and put it on his shoulder and started up the road. He had to sit down five times before he reached his shack.

Inside the shack he leaned the mast against the wall. In the dark he found a water bottle and took a drink. Then he lay down on the bed. He pulled the blanket over his shoulders and then over his back and legs and he slept face down on the newspapers with his arms out straight and the palms of his hands up.

He was asleep when the boy looked in the door in the morning. It was blowing so hard that the drifting boats would not be going out and the boy had slept late and then come to the old man's shack as he had come each morning. The boy saw that the old man was breathing and then he saw the old man's hands and he started to cry. He went out very quietly to go to bring some coffee and all the way down the road he was crying.

Many fishermen were around the skiff looking at what was lashed beside it and one was in the water, his trousers rolled up, measuring the skeleton with a length of line.

The boy did not go down. He had been there before and one of the fishermen was looking after the skiff for him.

'How is he?' one of the fishermen shouted.

'Sleeping,' the boy called. He did not care that they saw him crying. 'Let no one disturb him.'

'He was eighteen feet from nose to tail,' the fisherman who was measuring him called.

'I believe it,' the boy said.

He went into the Terrace and asked for a can of coffee.

'Hot and with plenty of milk and sugar in it.'

'Anything more?'

'No. Afterwards I will see what he can eat.'

'What a fish it was,' the proprietor said. 'There has never been such a fish. Those were two fine fish you took yesterday too.'

'Damn my fish,' the boy said and he started to cry again.

'Do you want a drink of any kind?' the proprietor asked.

'No,' the boy said. 'Tell them not to bother Santiago. I'll be back.'

'Tell him how sorry I am.'

'Thanks,' the boy said.

The boy carried the hot can of coffee up to the old man's shack and sat by him until he woke. Once it looked as though he were waking. But he had gone back into heavy sleep and the boy had gone across the road to borrow some wood to heat the coffee.

Finally the old man woke.

'Don't sit up,' the boy said. 'Drink this.' He poured some of the coffee in a glass.

The old man took it and drank it.

'They beat me, Manolin,' he said. 'They truly beat me.'

'*He* didn't beat you. Not the fish.'

'No. Truly. It was afterwards.'

'Pedrico is looking after the skiff and the gear. What do you want done with the head?'

'Let Pedrico chop it up to use in fish traps.'

'And the spear?'

'You keep it if you want it.'

'I want it,' the boy said. 'Now we must make our plans about the other things.'

'Did they search for me?'

'Of course. With coast guard and with planes.'

'The ocean is very big and a skiff is small and hard to see,' the old man said. He noticed how pleasant it was to have someone to talk to instead of speaking only to himself and to the sea. 'I missed you,' he said. 'What did you catch?'

'One the first day. One the second and two the third.'

'Very good.'

'Now we fish together again.'

'No. I am not lucky. I am not lucky any more.'

'The hell with luck,' the boy said. 'I'll bring the luck with me.'

'What will your family say?'

'I do not care. I caught two yesterday. But we will fish together now for I still have much to learn.'

'We must get a good killing lance and always have it on board. You can make the blade from a spring leaf from an old Ford. We can grind it in Guanabacoa. It should be sharp and not tempered so it will break. My knife broke.'

'I'll get another knife and have the spring ground.' How many days of heavy *brisa* have we?'

'Maybe three. Maybe more.'

'I will have everything in order,' the boy said. 'You get your hands well old man.'

'I know how to care for them. In the night I spat something strange and felt something in my chest was broken.'

'Get that well too,' the boy said. 'Lie down, old man, and I will bring you your clean shirt. And something to eat.'

'Bring any of the papers of the time that I was gone,' the old man said.

'You must get well fast for there is much that I can learn and you can teach me everything. How much did you suffer?'

'Plenty,' the old man said.

'I'll bring the food and the papers,' the boy said. 'Rest well, old man. I will bring stuff from the drugstore for your hands.'

'Don't forget to tell Pedrico the head is his.'

'No. I will remember.'

As the boy went out the door and down the worn coral rock road he was crying again.

That afternoon there was a party of tourists at the Terrace and looking down in the water among the empty beer cans and dead barracudas a woman saw a great long white spine with a huge tail at the end that lifted and swung with the tide while the east wind blew a heavy steady sea outside the entrance to the harbour.

'What's that?' she asked a waiter and pointed to the long backbone of the great fish that was now just garbage waiting to go out with the tide.

'Tiburon,' the waiter said. 'EShark.' He was meaning to explain what had happened.

'I didn't know sharks had such handsome, beautifully formed tails.'

'I didn't either,' her male companion said.

Up the road, in his shack, the old man was sleeping again. He was still sleeping on his face and the boy was sitting by him watching him. The old man was dreaming about the lions.

THE END

老人與海

Preface to the Chinese Translation
中文譯本序

一九五○年聖誕節後不久，海明威在古巴哈瓦那郊區他的別墅"觀景莊"動筆寫《老人與海》（起初名為《現有的海》，是一部寫"陸地、海洋與天空"的長篇小說[1]的第四也是結尾的部份），到一九五一年二月二十三日就完成了初稿，前後僅八週。四月份開始給去古巴訪問他的友人們傳閱，博得了一致的讚美。海明威本人也認為這是他"這一輩子所能寫的最好的一部作品"。由於原文全文僅兩萬六千多字，只好算是一篇中等長度的中篇小說，而且故事完全是獨立的，才考慮到單獨先發表的問題。利蘭·海沃德[2]建議請《生活》雜誌先在一期上刊出全文。一九五二年三月初，海明威寄出原稿時，在附致斯克里布納出版公司編輯的信中談到了這些打算，並說"現在發表《老人與海》可以駁倒認為我這個作家已經完蛋的那一派批評意見"[3]。原來在海明威上一部小說《渡河入林》發表後，評論家們評價不高，有的甚至很苛刻，認為他的文才已經枯竭了。

一九五二年九月，《生活》雜誌刊出了《老人與海》的全文，售出了五百三十一萬多份，後來的單行本也很快銷到了十萬冊。書評家和評論家們一致好評，親友及讀者紛紛來信祝賀。本書終於使海明威獲得了一九五三年度的普利茲獎金，並且主要由於它的成就而榮獲一九五四年度的諾貝爾文學獎。

《老人與海》的故事非常簡單，寫古巴老漁夫聖地亞哥在連續八十四天沒捕到魚的情況下，終於獨自釣上了一條大馬林魚，但這魚實在大，把他的小帆船在海上拖了三天才筋疲力盡，被他殺死了綁在小船的一邊，但在歸程中一再遭到鯊魚的襲擊，最後回港時只剩下魚頭魚尾和一條脊骨。這是根據真人真事寫的。一九三六年，海明威曾在《老爺》雜誌四月號上發表一篇不長的通訊，名為《在藍色海洋上》，就是報導這件事的。十五年後，他一氣呵成寫成了這部小說[4]，出版後評論家們就紛紛指出這簡單的故事富有象徵意味，是一則多層次的寓言。儘管海明威在一九五二年九月十三日致僑居意大利的美國藝術史家伯納德·貝倫森的信中寫道："沒有甚麼象徵主義的東西。大海就是大海，老人就是老人。男孩就是男孩，魚就是魚。鯊魚就是鯊魚……人們說甚麼象徵主義，全是胡說。"但他又說過："我試圖描寫一個真實的老人，一個真實的男孩，真實的大海，一條真實的魚和許多真實的鯊魚。然而，如果我能寫得足夠逼真的話，他們也能代表許多其他的事物。"[5]的確，從書中很多內證來看，作者顯然有意煞費苦心地把多層次的涵義融合在一個簡單的故事中。

首先，拿這故事本身來說，這是一曲英雄主義的讚歌。作者在這裏跳出了早期作品中的那個"人被一個敵意的宇宙毫無理由地懲罰"[6]的自然主義命題。《太陽依舊升起》中的傑克·巴恩斯在大戰中肉體受到創傷，不能像正常的人那樣跟他所愛的人相愛，最後只能認命，說一句："這麼想想不也很好嗎？"《永別了，武器》中的弗雷德里克·亨利，逃脫了戰火的摧殘，卻眼看愛人難產身亡，無能為力，只能像跟石像告別那樣離開了她的屍體，走向雨中。他們在厄運面前，至多表現得能"勇敢而富有風度地忍受"而已。老人聖地亞哥呢，儘管一開頭就處於不利的地位，八十四天沒捕到魚，認為"倒了血霉"，而別的漁夫都把他看作失敗者，他"消瘦憔悴"，手上有"勒得很深的傷疤"，沒錢買吃食，得靠那男孩給他送來，然而他的英勇正在於知其不可為而為之。在第八十五天，他決心"駛向遠方"去釣大魚。等到真的釣上了一條大馬林魚，明知對方力量比他強，還是決心戰鬥到底。"我跟你奉陪到死，"他說，因為當漁夫"正是我生來該做的事"。等到鯊魚一再來襲時，他用盡一切個人手段來反擊。魚叉被鯊魚帶走了，他把小刀綁在槳把上亂扎。刀子折斷了，他用短棍。短棍也丟掉了，他用舵把來打。儘管結果魚肉都被咬去了，但甚麼也無法摧殘他的英勇意志。老人在第一條鯊魚咬去了大約四十磅魚肉後想："然而人不是為失敗而生的，一個人可以被毀滅，但不能給打敗。"這句話道出了本書的主題。從這方面看，本書並不是甚麼寓言，而是一部現實主義的力作。海明威忠於他一貫的寫作方法，細緻地描寫人物的行動，諸如出海前的準備工作，出海後如何下餌，魚上鈎後如何跟牠周旋，最後如何把牠殺死了綁在船邊，以及如何和一條條鯊魚搏鬥的整個過程，都絲絲入扣地用白描手法細細道來，使這些外在的事件表現出內在的涵義，不用解釋，也無說教。正如作者本人所說："這本書描寫一個人的能耐可以達到甚麼程度，描寫人的心靈的尊嚴，而又沒有把心靈兩字用大寫字母標出來。"[7] 作者的手法在這裏確乎達到了完美的程度。

海明威在原來的故事中加了一個男孩。他五歲起就常陪老人一起出海釣魚。但這次老人是獨自出海的。他最後在深夜回進了港，繫好了小船，回窩棚摸黑上了牀。第二天早晨，男孩來找他，作者通過男孩的眼光，看見有個漁夫在量那死魚的殘骸，從鼻子到尾巴足足有十八英尺長，這一點烘托出老人這次捕魚活動是多麼了不起。隨後老人和男孩計劃用舊福特牌汽車的鋼板來改製魚叉的矛頭，再一同出海，這加強了本書的樂觀色彩，而老人的精神勝利還表現在末一句"老人正夢見獅子"中，因為作者在本書中屢次提到老人回憶年輕時看到非洲的海灘上有獅子出沒，通過獅子來代表旺盛的生命力和青春。

這男孩馬諾林除了用同情和崇拜來使讀者覺得老人的偉大以外，還提供了作者當時極感興趣的另一更複雜的主題：回歸。[8] 男孩帶回了老人失去的青春，使他見到他過去的自我。所以，獨自在海上的那三天裏，他口中經常唸着："但願那男孩在這裏就好了。"每說一遍，他就能重振精力來應付這艱苦的考驗。小獅子也起着同樣的作用，他"愛牠們，如同愛這男孩一樣"。

其次，這是一部希臘古典悲劇類型的作品。亞里士多德認為：悲劇主人公"之所以陷於厄運，不是由於他為非作惡，而是由於他犯了錯誤"[9]。老人聖地亞哥犯了一個致命的錯誤，那就是他常說的"我出海太遠了"。因為出海遠，才能釣上大魚，因為魚過份大，才被牠拖上三天，殺死後無法放在小船中，只能綁在一邊船舷外，於是在長途歸程中被鯊魚嗅到了血腥味，有充份的時間和空間來向死魚襲擊，把魚肉都咬掉，只剩下一副骨骸。這就是古典悲劇主人公所必然會受到的報應。所以當第一條鯊魚來襲時，作者寫道："這條鯊魚的出現不是偶然的。"鯊魚一到，老人和魚合而為一，同樣成了犧牲者。這是老人的意志和一切反對他的強大力量之間的搏鬥，而鯊魚正是宇宙間一切敵對力量的代表，成為復仇之神。這是不可避免的命運，而老人正是他自己的悲劇的製造者。

老人殺死了大魚，把它綁在船邊時，看來他是勝利了，但他知道要有報應。所以他說過："如果有鯊魚來，願天主憐憫牠［指這條大魚］和我吧。"這捕魚的經過，加上後來老人和鯊魚搏鬥的過程，就是亞里士多德關於悲劇的定義"悲劇是對於一個嚴肅、完整、有一定長度的行動的摹仿"[10]中所說的行動。而殺死大魚後更清楚地顯示了他這行動是犯了致命的錯誤，他必然要受到懲罰。

同時，根據黑格爾在《美學》一書中所述，"悲劇行動的真正內容，是由存在於人的願望之中的一些實體性的、自身合理的力量所提供的。這些力量決定悲劇人物追求的各種目的。"[11]"於是個人的行動，在特定情況之下，力求實現某一目的……勢必會引起和它對立的激情來反對自己，因而導致難以避免的衝突。"[12]所以本書又可被看作兩個致命而彼此衝突的目的或存在的悲劇。那大魚也是這悲劇中的一個主人公，牠失敗了，被殺了，但是還得遭到鯊魚的殘害。老人看來勝利了，但知道要受到報應。整個搏鬥過程中，老人明明知道雙方都在絕對忠誠地履行自己的職責。"牠選擇的是待在黑暗的深水裏，遠遠地避開一切圈套、羅網和詭計。我選擇的是趕到誰也沒到過的地方去找牠。""不過牠似乎很鎮靜，他想，而且在按着牠的計劃行動。"正因為老人對魚的行動理解得這麼清楚，他才對牠懷有複雜的感情。一方面是"你要把我害死啦，魚啊，老人想。不過你有權利這樣做"，但另一方面卻接着這樣想：“我從沒見過比你更龐大、更美麗、更沉着或更崇高的東西，老弟。來，把我害死吧。我不在乎誰害死誰。”但接着就埋怨起自己來了：“你現在頭腦糊塗起來啦。”因為儘管“這條魚也是我的朋友……不過我必須把牠弄死”。他所追求的目的是絕不動搖的。

本書中援引了不少關於基督受難的細節，説明作者有意識地把老人比作基督的化身，在故事的全過程中經歷了兩次被釘十字架的過程。第一次是老人釣上了大魚時開始的，他和小船被魚拖着走，把釣索勒在背上，感到疼痛（喻指耶穌扛着十字架上髑髏地 [13]），才用一個蔴袋襯墊在釣索下（耶穌身上穿着袍子），而緊扣在頭上的草帽把額部勒得好痛（耶穌頭上戴着荊冠），雙手被釣索勒得出血（耶穌手上釘着釘子）。而出海前男孩給他送來的吃食，喻指耶穌的“最後晚餐”。

第二次被釘上十字架的過程，是從鯊魚來襲時開始的。他用魚叉扎死了第一條來犯的鯊魚。後來，等他看到另兩條鯊魚中首先露面的那一條時，不禁“Ay”了一聲。作者描述道：“這個詞是沒法翻譯的，也許不過是一聲叫喊，就像一個人覺得釘子穿過他的雙手，釘進木頭時不由自主地發出的聲音。”這不是明白無誤地表示老人又被釘上了十字架嗎？

再說，聖地亞哥這名字是雅各在西班牙語中的拼法。雅各原是個漁夫，是耶穌在加利利海濱最早收的四門徒之一。所以老人同時也具有耶穌的門徒或一般謀求聖職的信徒的身份。他在釣魚過程中一再吃生魚肉，喝水，這喻指信徒領聖餐。魚肉代表聖餅，基督的肉體。老人一聲聲叫喚那偉大的棒球明星迪馬喬的名字，拿他當聖徒看待。最後老人回到家，摸黑躺下。作者寫道："他臉朝下躺在報紙上，兩臂伸得筆直，手掌向上。"耐人尋味的是海明威沒有寫明這兩臂是朝上伸出（這是教士領受聖職時的姿勢），還是向兩旁伸出（這是基督被釘十字架的姿勢）。作者分明暗示這主人公是人又是神，兼有人性和神性的雙重身份。

本書開頭時提到老人曾一度八十七天沒捕到魚。根據耶穌的事蹟和基督教的節期來看，這個數字似乎含有深意在內。按耶穌受洗後，曾被聖靈引到曠野，禁食四十晝夜，受到魔鬼的試探。[14]（本書開頭描寫老人雙手上由於用繩索拉大魚而留下的刻得很深的傷疤時，作者特意寫道："它們像無魚可打的沙漠中被侵蝕的地方一般古老。"這無魚可打的沙漠即喻指"曠野"。）這四十天加上基督教大齋期的四十天再加上復活節前的"聖週"那七天，剛好是八十七天。這次老人在海上一連八十四天沒打到魚，接下來在海上待了三天，剛好等於基督從受難到復活那三天。老人在這三天中經歷了大磨難，最後獲得精神勝利。

這兩個八十七天的過程，似乎表明了人生是循環的，是無休止的一系列被釘上十字架的過程。以前發生過，現在重複經歷，今後還是會不斷發生。老人聖地亞哥代表着所有的人的形象，經受着最強烈的放之四海而皆準的苦難的歷程。這是符合海明威把人生看作是一場悲劇的觀點的。

另一方面，這大馬林魚被釣上了，在拖着船走的過程中，被嘴裏的釣鈎勒得好痛。這時魚也成了基督的化身。所以老人自言自語地說："你現在覺得痛了吧，魚，老實說，我也是如此啊。"他不禁替牠感到傷心，並且認為牠"也是我的朋友"。等到把它綁在船邊，在歸航途中遇到鯊魚一再襲擊時，這雙重基督的形象是再明顯不過的了。

為了突出人生是一系列被釘上十字架的過程，作者在最後寫到老人獨自深夜返港，背起捲着帆的桅桿爬上岸去，一再摔倒在地（這一點又和傳說中耶穌背着十字架上髑髏地時跌倒的故事交相輝映），第二天男孩來看他時，老人提起夜間"吐出了一些奇怪的東西，感到胸膛裏有甚麼東西碎了"，這是暗示基督被羅馬兵丁用長矛刺身，流出血水來。而最最生動的一點是老人扛起桅桿時，曾回頭望那綁在船邊的魚的殘骸。這一個靜止的鏡頭顯示老人作為一個基督，正在開始另一次苦難的歷程，而那魚作為另一個基督，正綁在十字架上。作者就這樣把上十字架的全過程濃縮在一起了：基督上髑髏地、基督被綁在十字架上、基督死去。這着重指出了所有生物的共同命運是一系列上十字架的磨難。而那條大魚的殘骸，作者最後描寫道："它如今僅僅是垃圾，只等潮水來把它帶走了。"這等於暗示，所有物質的東西，包括人在內，都是註定要毀滅的，只有人的行動，和對行動的記憶才是永存的。所以全書的末一句是："老人正夢見獅子。"他保持着完好的對事物的記憶。

最後，《老人與海》作為寓言，還闡明了海明威對作家和寫作的看法。文中用多方面的象徵比喻來表達他本人創作生涯的種種細節，完整地說明了藝術家的艱苦的創作過程。作者把漁夫比作作家，捕魚術代表寫作藝術，而大魚則是偉大的作品。作為這個性質的寓言，海明威寫得層次分明。下面且來一層層地說明。

首先，作家應離羣索居，鍥而不捨。海明威在諾貝爾文學獎授獎儀式上的《書面發言》中說，"寫作，在最成功的時候，是一種孤寂的生涯。" [15] 所以，《老人與海》開端第一句就是："他是個獨自在灣流中一條平底小帆船上釣魚的老人。"而作家的使命正是寫作，不能想別的（因為當漁夫"正是我生來該做的事"），而且只能靠自己（大魚把船拖着走後，老人時刻想到有男孩在該多好，但事實上是不可能有人來幫助他），必須完成這傑作（和魚搏鬥，寧死不屈），等到發現這傑作的偉大（他第一次看見魚長長的身影時，還不大相信竟會那麼大），更堅定了完成的決心（殺死了綁在小船一邊），事後依舊保持着對創作的忠誠，轉向新的挑戰（鯊魚一次次來襲），要全力保衛它，但一次次的努力都無濟於事（無法不讓評論家來糟蹋），最後儘管感到哀傷，傑作被毀，但獲得了一個崇高的悲劇英雄的幸福感，知道這偉大的創作永遠是屬於他的。

其次，作者用釣魚術的細緻描寫來印證技巧的重要性：出海前仔細準備（平時小心保藏釣魚的工具，小心準備魚餌，把備用的那幾圈釣索連接在一起），使四根釣索保持在正確的深度和位置上，比別人更精確。而技巧和靈感的關係可以從作者對老人的雙手的描繪上看出。剛釣上這大魚時，他的左手抽起筋來。老人不禁責怪起這隻手來，並連連吃生魚肉，盼望它早點復原來幫助他的右手。有一條諺語說："左手是個夢想者。"它代表着靈感，是虛弱而難以捉摸的，所以老人認為這左手的抽筋"是對自己身體的背叛行為……是丟自己的臉，尤其是一個人的時候"。右手則是又堅強又忠誠，代表着訓練有素的寫作技巧。他當初在卡薩布蘭卡一家酒店裏跟那個大個子黑人比手勁時，堅持了一天一夜，最後就是靠那隻右手取勝而贏得"冠軍"這外號的。

在創作過程中，藝術家和藝術品逐漸合二為一。老人把魚綁好在小船一邊，在歸程中想道：“我們像親兄弟一樣航行着。……是它在帶我回家，還是我在帶它回家呢？”這說明這時他和死魚已成為一體，傑作成為作家的一部份了。所以當鯊魚摧殘死魚時，老人“感到就像自己挨到襲擊一樣”。而傑作的命運正跟這死魚的一樣，總要受到摧殘，只有藝術家心明眼亮，早看出了這一點，但又明白只要完成了傑作，它就成為一個既成的事實，將經得起時間的考驗，永存在人們的記憶中。

對待這種傑作，不同的人有不同的態度。作家中有些同行，將理解它的重要意義正在於為他們樹立了榜樣，給他們以啟示。有個漁夫量了這死魚的殘骸，叫道：“它從鼻子到尾巴有十八英尺長。”這使在場的漁夫們認識到老人這場搏鬥的艱巨，受到磨難之深。而另外有些不知好歹的人，卻附和着批評家的意見，用言語來糟蹋傑作。本書最末頁上，作者特意通過一旅遊者之口，說甚麼“我不知道鯊魚有這樣漂亮的、形狀這樣美觀的尾巴”。她把大馬林魚的殘骸錯當為鯊魚時，混淆了是非，把破壞傑作者當成傑作本身，竟反而尊崇破壞者。這是個莫大的嘲弄。

一個作家對事物的遠見，海明威認為是最最重要的，是作品的來源。在本書中他以獅子為象徵。老人開頭時處於失敗的境地，被人蔑視，靠夢見獅子來做精神支持，在磨難最難熬的關頭，他想，“但願牠[指那大魚]睡去，這樣我也能睡去，夢見獅子。”後來，在海上最後一個夜間，他終於睡着了，又夢見了獅子。作者就是用這種形象來說明藝術家必須保持個人的遠見。他在《書面發言》中寫道：“一個在岑寂中獨立工作的作家，假若他確實不同凡響，就必須天天面對永恆的東西……"

在本書中，鯊魚主要代表一切破壞性的力量：被人蔑視、忽視，缺乏自信以及悲觀絕望等等。鯊魚也泛指書評家和評論家，但作者對他們是區別對待的。他最痛恨的是那種"食腐肉的"鯊魚，因為牠們"朝魚身上被咬過的地方咬"。這是指那種人云亦云的評論家，他們全是懦夫。但作者對首先來襲的那條大灰鯖鯊，卻說牠"生就一副好體格，能游得跟海裏最快的魚一般快，周身的一切都很美……"。"牠不是食腐動物……牠是美麗而崇高的，見甚麼都不怕。"這是指那種有真知灼見的偉大的評論家，和偉大的作家匹配，同樣偉大。這種真正的評論有益於作家對事物的遠見，正如那老人跟大多數漁夫不同，並不厭惡鯊魚肝油的味道，因為他知道喝了"對眼睛也有好處"。

最後，作者還通過書中一些細節描寫，闡明了藝術家在創作傑作的過程中如何維持生計的問題。老人出海前男孩送來食物，在海上和大魚搏鬥的過程中一次次吃生魚肉，都強調了物質條件和經濟條件的重要性。肉體必須得到營養，腦力勞動才能進行。海明威在文學生涯中常靠新聞寫作來貼補生活。他在本書中用捕海龜的活動來比作新聞寫作。聖地亞哥早年曾在尼加拉瓜東部海岸外捉過多年海龜，為了長力氣，他常吃白色的海龜蛋，"在五月份連吃了整整一個月，使自己到九、十月份能身強力壯，去捕真正的大魚"。這是說搞新聞寫作不但能使自己活得下去，也能給他以磨練，去創作地道的傑作。在這方面他是有過顧慮的。在一九三八年發表的《〈第五縱隊〉與首輯四十九篇》的前言中，海明威寫道："在你不得不去必須去的地方，不得不做必須做的工作，並且不得不看你必須看的事物的過程中，你把你用來寫作的工具弄鈍。"但是弄鈍的工具可以重新磨快。主要還得靠寫作實踐。所以那男孩説："你……捕了好多年海龜，你的眼力還是挺好的嘛。"這裏，眼力是指作家對事物的觀察力和遠見而言。實際上老人是長於此道的。"他對海龜並不抱着神秘的看法。"這等於説海明威能現實地對待報紙和雜誌上的新聞寫作。他蔑視一般平庸的新聞寫作（"他還對那又大又笨的蠵龜抱着不懷惡意的輕蔑……"），讚美他好友們的出色的報導文章（"他喜歡綠色的海龜和玳瑁，牠們形態優美，游水迅速，價值很高……"）。

綜上所述，《老人與海》在短短的篇幅中融合了如此複雜的層次，把它們交織在一起，可以説做到了渾然一體，天衣無縫。作者是頗有自知之明的。他在交稿時致出版社編輯的信中不但提起"這是我這一輩子所能寫的最好的一部作品"，還説本書"可以作為我全部創作的尾聲，作為我寫作、生活中已經學到或者想學的那一切的尾聲"。這話不幸而言中了。從當時直到一九六一年七月二日自殺，海明威再沒有發表過甚麼重要的作品。

英國當代著名小説家、評論家安東尼・伯吉斯在一九八四年發表的《現代小説：九十九本佳作》中關於《老人與海》寫過下列這幾句話："這個樸素的故事裏充滿了並非故意賣弄的寓意……作為一篇乾淨利落的'陳述性'散文，它在海明威的全部作品中都是無與倫比的。每一個詞都有它的作用，沒有一個詞是多餘的。"[16] 這看法似乎並不言過其實。

吳勞

註解

1 該小說的前三部的原稿，在海明威自殺身亡後，由其妻子瑪麗・威爾士及斯克里布納出版公司的小查理斯・斯克里布納共同整理，於 1970 年出版，書名《島在灣流中》。

2 利蘭・海沃德為百老匯戲劇演出人及好萊塢製片人，後來以十五萬美元買下《老人與海》的攝製權，於 1958 年公映。

3 這一頁上的兩段引文分別引自《海明威談創作》（董衡巽編選，三聯書店，1985 年）第 140 及第 141 至 142 頁。

4 本書最後出版的定本幾乎就是一年半前在海明威親朋中傳閱的手稿，改動是不多的。

5 引自《時代》雜誌，1954 年 12 月 13 日。

6 見沃特・威廉斯著《歐內斯特・海明威的悲劇寫作藝術》（路易斯安那州立大學出版社，1981 年）第 174 頁。

7 引自《海明威談創作》第 143 頁。

8 參見卡洛斯・貝克：《老人與海》前言（斯克里布納出版公司，1962 年）。

9 引自《西方文論選》（伍蠡甫主編，上海譯文出版社，1979 年）上卷第 68 至 69 頁。

10 引自《西方文論選》上卷第 57 頁。

11 引自《西方文論選》下卷第 306 頁。

12 同上，第 308 頁。

13 參見《聖經・約翰福音》第 19 章第 17 節。

14 參見《聖經・馬太福音》第 4 章第 1 至 11 節。

15 引自《海明威談創作》第 25 頁。

16 引自《世界文學》1985 年第 3 期第 286 頁。

獻給
查理斯・斯克里布納和
麥克斯・柏金斯[1]

他是個獨自在灣流[2]中一條平底小帆船上釣魚的老人，這一次已去了八十四天，沒捕到一條魚。頭四十天裏，有個男孩跟他在一起。可是過了四十天還沒捉到一條魚，男孩的父母對他説，老人如今一定是終於"倒了血霉"，這就是説，倒霉到了極點，於是男孩聽從了他們的吩咐，上了另外一條船，頭一個禮拜就捕到了三條好魚。男孩看見老人每天回來時船總是空的，感到很難受，他總是走下岸去，幫老人拿捲起的釣索，或者魚鈎和魚叉，還有收捲在桅桿上的帆。帆上用麵粉袋片打了些補丁，收攏後看來像是一面標誌着永遠失敗的旗子。

老人消瘦憔悴，脖頸上有些很深的皺紋。腮幫上有些褐斑，那是太陽在熱帶海面上的反光所造成的良性皮膚病變。褐斑從他臉的兩側一直蔓延下去，他的雙手常用繩索拉大魚，留下了勒得很深的傷疤。但是這些傷疤中沒有一塊是新的。它們像無魚可打的沙漠中被侵蝕的地方一般古老。

他身上的一切都顯得古老，除了那雙眼睛，它們像海水一般藍，顯得喜洋洋而不服輸。

"聖地亞哥，"他們從小船停泊的地方爬上岸時，男孩對他說。"我又能陪你出海了。我家掙到了一點錢。"

老人教會了這男孩捕魚，男孩愛他。

"不，"老人說。"你遇上了一條交好運的船。跟他們待下去吧。"

"不過你該記得，你有一次八十七天釣不到一條魚，跟着有三個禮拜，我們每天都捕到了大魚。"

"我記得，"老人說。"我知道你不是因為沒把握才離開我的。"

"是爸爸叫我走的。我是孩子，不能不聽他的。"

"我明白，"老人說。"這合情合理。"

"他沒多大的信心。"

"是啊，"老人說。"可是我們有。可不是嗎？"

"對，"男孩說。"我請你到露台飯店³去喝杯啤酒，然後一起把打魚的工具帶回去。"

"那好啊，"老人說。"都是打魚人嘛。"

他們坐在飯店前的露台上，不少漁夫拿老人開玩笑，老人並不生氣。另外一些上了些年紀的漁夫望着他，感到難受。不過他們並不流露出來，只是斯文地談起海流，他們把釣索送到海面下有多深，天氣一貫多麼好，還談起他們的見聞。當天打魚得手的漁夫都已回來，把大馬林魚剖開，整片橫排在兩塊木板上，每塊木板的兩端各由兩個人抬着，搖搖晃晃地送到收魚站，在那裏等冷藏車來把它們運往哈瓦那的市場。捕到鯊魚的人們已把它們送到海灣另一邊的鯊魚加工廠去，吊在組合滑車上，除去肝臟，割掉魚鰭，剝去外皮，把魚肉切成一條條，以備醃製。

颳東風的時候，鯊魚加工廠隔着海灣送來一股腥味；但今天只有淡淡的一絲，因為風轉向了北方，後來逐漸平息，飯店露台上可人心意、陽光明媚。

"聖地亞哥，"男孩說。

"哦，"老人說。他正握着酒杯，思量好多年前的事情。

"要我去弄點沙甸魚來給你明天用嗎？"

"不。打棒球去吧。我划船還行，羅赫略會給我撒網的。"

"我很想去。即使不能陪你釣魚，我也很想給你多少做點事。"

"你請我喝了杯啤酒，"老人說。"你已經是個大人啦。"

"你頭一次帶我上船，我有多大？"

"五歲，那天我把一條鮮龍活跳的魚拖上船去，牠差一點把船撞得粉碎，你也差一點給送了命。還記得嗎？"

"我記得魚尾巴砰砰地拍着，船上的座板給打斷了，還有棍子打魚的聲音。我記得你把我朝船頭猛推，那裏攔着濕漉漉的釣索卷，我感到整條船在顫抖，聽到你啪啪地用棍子打魚的聲音，像在砍倒一棵樹，還記得我渾身上下都是甜絲絲的血腥味。"

"你當真記得那回事，還是我不久前剛跟你說過？"

"打從我們頭一次一起出海時起，甚麼事情我都記得清清楚楚。"

老人用他那雙常遭日曬而目光堅定的眼睛愛憐地望着他。

"如果你是我自己的小子,我一定會帶你出去闖一下,"他說。"可你是你爸爸和你媽媽的小子,你搭的又是一條交上了好運的船。"

"我去弄沙甸魚來好嗎?我還知道上哪裏去弄四份大魚餌來。"

"我今天還有自己剩下的。我把它們放在匣子裏醃了。"

"我給你弄四條新鮮的來吧。"

"一條,"老人說。他的希望和他的信心從沒消失過。這時可又像微風初起時那麼鮮活了。

"兩條,"男孩說。

"就兩條吧,"老人同意了。"你不是去偷的吧?"

"我願意去偷,"男孩說。"不過這些是買來的。"

"謝謝你了,"老人說。他心地單純,不去捉摸自己甚麼時候達到這樣謙卑的地步。可是他知道這時正達到了這地步,知道這並不丟臉,所以也無損於真正的自尊心。

"看這海流,明天會是個好日子,"他說。

"你打算去哪裏?"男孩問。

"駛到遠方,等轉了風才回來。我想不等天亮就出發。"

"我要想辦法叫船主人也駛到遠方,"男孩說。"這樣,如果你釣到了真正大的魚,我們可以趕去幫你的忙。"

"他可不會願意駛到很遠的地方。"

"是啊,"男孩說。"不過我會看見一些他看不見的東西,比如說有隻鳥在空中盤旋,我就會叫他趕去追海豚[4]的。"

"他眼睛這麼不行嗎？"

"差不多瞎了。"

"這可怪了，"老人說。"他從沒捕過海龜。這玩意才會把眼睛毀了。"

"你可在莫斯基托海岸[5]外捕了好多年海龜，你的眼力還是挺好的嘛。"

"我是個不同尋常的老頭。"

"不過你現在還有力氣對付一條真正大的魚嗎？"

"我想還有。再說有不少竅門可用呢。"

"我們把工具拿回家去吧，"男孩說。"這樣我可以拿了撒網去捉沙甸魚。"

他們從船上拿起打魚的工具。老人把桅桿扛上肩頭，男孩拿着內放編得很緊密的褐色釣索卷的木箱、魚鈎和帶桿子的魚叉。盛魚餌的匣子給藏在小帆船的船梢下面，那裏還有那根在大魚被拖到船邊時用來收服牠們的棍子。誰也不會來偷老人的東西，不過還是把船帆和那些粗釣索帶回家去的好，因為露水對這些東西不利，再說，儘管老人深信當地不會有人來偷他的東西，但他認為，把一把魚鈎和一支魚叉留在船上實在是不必要的引誘。

他們順着大路一起走到老人的窩棚，從敞開的門走進去。老人把繞着帆的桅桿靠在牆上，男孩把木箱和其他工具擱在它的旁邊。桅桿跟這單間的窩棚差不多一般長。窩棚用叫做 guano 的王棕[6]的堅韌的護芽棕皮做成，裏面有一張牀、一張桌子、一把椅子和泥地上一處用木炭燒飯的地方。在用這纖維結實的被展平的棕葉疊蓋而成的褐色牆壁上，有一幅彩色的耶穌聖心圖[7]和另一幅科夫萊聖母圖[8]。這是他妻子的遺物。牆上一度掛着一幅他妻子的着色照,但他把它取下了,因為看了使他覺得太孤單,它如今在屋角擱板上他那件乾淨襯衫下面。

"有甚麼吃的東西?"男孩問。

"有鍋魚煮黃米飯。要吃點嗎?"

"不。我回家去吃。要我給你生火嗎?"

"不用。等會我自己來生。也許就吃冷飯算了。"

"我把撒網拿去好嗎?"

"當然好。"

其實並沒有魚網,男孩還記得他們是甚麼時候把它賣掉的。然而他們每天都要扯一套這種謊話。也沒有一鍋魚煮黃米飯,這一點男孩也知道。

"八十五是個吉利的數目,"老人説。"你可想看到我捕回來一條去掉了下腳有一千多磅重的魚?"

"我拿撒網撈沙甸魚去。你坐在門口曬曬太陽可好?"

"好吧。我有張昨天的報紙,我來看看棒球消息。"

男孩不知道昨天的報紙是不是也是想像出來的。但是老人把它從牀下取出來了。

"佩里科在酒館裏給我的,"他解釋説。

"我弄到了沙甸魚就回來。我要把你的魚跟我的一起用冰鎮着,明天早上就可以分着用了。等我回來了,你給我講講棒球消息。"

"洋基隊[9]不會輸。"

"可是我怕克里夫蘭印第安人隊會贏。"

“相信洋基隊吧，好孩子。別忘了那了不起的迪馬喬[10]。”

“我擔心底特律老虎隊，也擔心克里夫蘭印第安人隊。”

“當心點，要不然連辛辛那提紅人隊和芝加哥白襪隊，你都要擔心啦。”

“你好好看報，等我回來了給我講講。”

“你看我們該去買張末尾是八五的彩票嗎？明天是第八十五天。”

“這樣做行啊，”男孩說。“不過你上次創的紀錄是八十七天，這怎麼說？”

“這種事情不會再發生。你看能弄到一張末尾是八五的嗎？”

“我可以去訂一張。”

“訂一張。這要兩塊半。我們向誰去借這筆錢呢？”

“這個容易。我總能借到兩塊半的。”

“我看可能我也借得到。不過我不想借錢。第一步是借錢。下一步就要討飯囉。”

“穿得暖和點，老大爺，”男孩說。“別忘了，我們這是在九月裏。”

“正是大魚露面的月份，”老人說。“在五月裏，人人都能當個好漁夫的。”

“我現在去撈沙甸魚，”男孩說。

等男孩回來的時候，老人在椅子上熟睡着，太陽已經下去了。男孩從牀上撿起條舊軍毯，鋪在椅背上，蓋住了老人的雙肩。這兩個肩膀挺怪，人非常老邁了，肩膀卻依然很強健，脖子也依然很壯實，而且當老人睡着了，腦袋向前垂着的時候，皺紋也不大明顯了。他的襯衫上不知打了多少次補丁，弄得像他那張帆一樣，而這些補丁被陽光曬得褪成了許多深淺不同的顏色。老人的頭非常蒼老，眼睛閉上了，臉上就一點生氣也沒有。那報紙攤在他膝蓋上，在晚風中，靠他一條胳臂壓着才沒被吹走。他光着腳。

男孩撇下老人走了，等他回來時，老人還是熟睡着。

"醒來吧，老大爺，"男孩說，一手搭上老人的膝蓋。

老人張開眼睛，他的神志一時彷彿正在從老遠的地方回來。隨後他微笑了。

"你拿來了甚麼？"他問。

"晚飯，"男孩說。"我們來吃吧。"

"我還不大餓。"

"來吃吧。你不能只打魚，不吃飯。"

"我這麼做過，"老人說着，站起身來，拿起報紙，把它摺好。跟着他動手摺疊毯子。

"把毯子披在身上吧，"男孩說。"只要我活着，你就決不會不吃飯就去打魚。"

"這麼說，祝你長壽，多保重自己吧，"老人說。"我們吃甚麼？"

"黑豆米飯、油炸香蕉 [11]，還有些燉菜。"

男孩是把這些飯菜放在雙層白鐵飯匣裏從露台飯店拿來的。他口袋裏有兩副刀叉和湯匙，每一副都用紙餐巾包着。

"這是誰給你的？"

"馬丁。那老闆。"

"我得去謝謝他。"

"我已經謝過啦，"男孩說。"你用不着去謝他了。"

"我要給他一塊大魚肚子上的肉，"老人說。"他這樣幫助我們不止一次了？"

"我想是這樣吧。"

"這樣的話，我該在魚肚子肉以外，再送他一些東西。他對我們真關心。"

"他還送了兩瓶啤酒。"

"我喜歡罐裝的啤酒。"

"我知道。不過這是瓶裝的，阿圖依牌 [12] 啤酒，我還得把瓶子送回去呢。"

"你真周到，"老人說。"我們該吃了吧？"

"我一直在要你吃哪，"男孩和氣地對他說。"不等你準備好，我是不願打開飯匣子的。"

"我現在準備好了，"老人說。"我不過要點時間洗洗手臉。"

你上哪裏去洗呢？男孩想。村裏的公用水龍頭在大路上過去第二條橫路的轉角上。我該為他把水帶到這裏來，男孩想，還帶塊肥皂和一條乾淨毛巾。我為甚麼這樣粗心大意？我該再給他弄件襯衫，一件過冬的茄克衫，還弄雙甚麼鞋子，再來條毯子。

"你拿來的燉菜太好吃了，"老人說。

"給我講講棒球賽吧，"男孩請求他說。

"在美國聯賽 [13] 中，總是洋基隊的天下，我跟你說過啦，"老人興高采烈地說。

"他們今天輸了，"男孩告訴他。

"這算不上甚麼。那了不起的迪馬喬恢復他的本色了。"

"他們隊裏還有別的好手哪。"

"這還用說。不過有了他就不同了。在另一個聯賽[14]中,布魯克林隊對費城隊,我看布魯克林隊穩贏。不過我還惦念着狄克·西斯勒和他在那老公園[15]裏打出的那些好球。"

"這些好球從來沒有別人打過。我見過的擊球中,數他打得最遠。"

"你還記得他過去常來露台飯店嗎?我很想陪他出海釣魚,可我膽子太小,不敢對他開口。所以我要你去說,可你也膽子太小。"

"我記得。那是個大錯。他挺有可能跟我們一起出海的。這樣,我們就可以一輩子記得這回事了。"

"我很想陪那了不起的迪馬喬去釣魚,"老人說。"人家說他父親也是個打魚的。也許他當初也像我們這樣窮,會理解我們的。"

"那了不起的西斯勒的爸爸[16]從沒過過窮日子,而他,他爸爸,像我這個年紀就在大聯賽裏打球了。"

"我像你這個年紀,就在一條去非洲的橫帆船上當普通水手了,我見過獅子在傍晚到海灘上來。"

"我知道。你跟我談起過。"

"我們來談非洲還是談棒球?"

"我看談棒球吧,"男孩說。"給我談談那了不起的約翰·J·麥格勞[17]的情況。"他把這個 J 唸成"何塔"[18]。

"在過去的日子裏,他有時候也常到露台飯店來。可是他一喝了酒，就態度粗暴，出口傷人，難以相處。他腦子裏想着棒球，也想着賽馬。至少他老是口袋裏揣着賽馬的名單，常常在電話裏提到一些馬匹的名字。"

"他是個偉大的經理，"男孩説。"我爸爸認為他是最偉大的。"

"這是因為他來這裏的次數最多，"老人説。"要是杜洛奇[19]繼續每年來這裏，你爸爸就會認為他是最偉大的經理了。"

"説真的，誰是最偉大的經理，盧克[20]還是邁克·岡薩雷茲[21]？"

"我認為他們不相上下。"

"可最棒的漁夫是你。"

"不。我知道還有比我強的。"

"哪裏，"男孩説。"好漁夫很多，還有些很了不起的。不過只有你是獨一無二的。"

"謝謝你。你説得叫我高興。我希望不要來一條大魚，大得能證明我們都講錯啦。"

"這樣的魚是沒有的，只要你還是像你説的那樣強壯。"

"我也許不像我自以為的那樣強壯了，"老人説。"可是我懂得不少竅門，而且有決心。"

"你該馬上去睡覺，這樣明天早上才精神飽滿。我要把這些東西送回露台飯店。"

"那麼祝你晚安。早上我去叫醒你。"

"你是我的鬧鐘，"男孩説。

"年紀是我的鬧鐘，"老人説。"為甚麼老頭醒得那麼早？難道是要讓白天長些嗎？"

"我不知道，"男孩説。"我只知道少年睡得沉，起得晚。"

"我記在心上，"老人説。"到時候會去叫醒你的。"

"我不願讓船主人來叫醒我。這樣似乎我比他差勁了。"

"我懂。"

"安睡吧，老大爺。"

男孩走出屋去。他們剛才吃飯的時候，桌子上沒點燈，老人就脱了長褲，摸黑上了牀。他把長褲捲起來當枕頭，把那張報紙塞在裏頭。他用毯子裹住了身子，在彈簧墊上鋪着的其他舊報紙上睡下了。

他不多久就睡熟了，夢見小時候見到的非洲，長長的金色海灘和白色海灘，白得耀眼，還有高聳的海岬和褐色的大山。他如今每天夜裏都神遊那道海岸，在夢中聽見拍岸海浪的隆隆聲，看見土人駕船穿浪而行。他睡着時聞到甲板上柏油和填絮[22]的氣味，還聞到早晨陸地上颳來的微風帶來的非洲氣息。

通常一聞到陸地上颳來的微風，他就醒來，穿上衣服去叫醒那男孩。然而今夜陸地上颳來的微風的氣息來得很早，他在夢中知道時間尚早，就繼續把夢做下去，看見羣島間那些白色浪峯從海面上升起，隨後夢見了加那利羣島[23]的各個港灣和錨泊地。

他不再夢見風暴，不再夢見婦女們，不再夢見發生過的大事，不再夢見大魚，不再夢見打架，不再夢見角力，不再夢見他的妻子。他如今只夢見某些地方和海灘上的獅子。牠們在暮色中像小貓一般嬉耍着，他愛牠們，如同愛這男孩一樣。他從沒夢見過這男孩。他就這麼醒過來，望望敞開的門外邊的月亮，攤開長褲穿上。他在窩棚外撒了尿，然後順着大路走去叫醒男孩。他被清晨的寒氣弄得直哆嗦。但他知道哆嗦了一陣後會感到暖和，用不了多久就要去划船了。

男孩住的那所房子的門沒有上鎖，他推開門，光着腳悄悄走進去。男孩在外間一張帆布牀上熟睡着，老人靠着外面射進來的殘月的光線，清楚地看見他。他輕輕握住男孩的一隻腳，直到男孩醒來，轉過臉來對他望着。老人點點頭，男孩從牀邊椅子上拿起他的長褲，坐在牀沿上穿褲子。

老人走出門去，男孩跟在他背後。他還是昏昏欲睡，老人伸出胳臂摟住他的肩膀說，"對不起。"

"哪裏！"男孩說。"男子漢就該這麼做。

他們順着大路朝老人的窩棚走去，一路上，有些光着腳的男人在黑暗中走動，扛着他們船上的桅桿。

他們走進老人的窩棚，男孩拿起裝在籃子裏的釣索卷，還有魚叉和魚鈎，老人把繞着帆的桅桿扛在肩上。

"想喝咖啡嗎？"男孩問。

"我們把工具放在船裏，然後喝一點吧。"

他們在一家清早就營業的供應漁夫的小吃館裏，喝着盛在煉乳罐頭裏的咖啡。

"你睡得怎麼樣，老大爺？"男孩問。他如今清醒過來了，儘管要他完全擺脫睡魔還不大容易。

"睡得很好，馬諾林，"老人說。"我感到今天挺有把握。"

"我也這樣，"男孩說。"現在我該去拿你我用的沙甸魚，還有給你的新鮮魚餌。那條船上的打魚工具總是他自己拿的。他從來不要別人幫他拿東西。"

"我們可不同,"老人説。"你還只五歲時我就讓你幫忙拿東西了。"

"我記得,"男孩説。"我馬上回來。再要杯咖啡吧。我們在這裏可以賒賬。"

他走了,光着腳在珊瑚石砌的走道上向保藏魚餌的冷藏所走去。

老人慢騰騰地喝着咖啡。這是他今天一整天的飲食,他知道應該把它喝了。好久以來,吃飯使他感到厭煩,因此從來不帶午飯。他在小帆船的船頭上放着一瓶水,一整天只需要這個就夠了。

男孩這時帶着沙甸魚和兩份包在報紙裏的魚餌回來了,他們就順着小徑走向小帆船,感到腳下的沙地裏嵌着鵝卵石,他們抬起小帆船,讓它溜進水裏。

"祝你好運,老大爺。"

"祝你好運,"老人説。他把槳上的繩圈套在槳座的釘子上,身子朝前衝,抵消槳片在水中所遇到的阻力,在黑暗中動手划出港去。其他那些海灘上也有其他船隻在出海,老人聽到他們的槳落水和划動的聲音,儘管此刻月亮已掉到了山背後,他還看不清他們。

偶爾有條船上有人在説話。但是除了槳聲外,大多數船隻都寂靜無聲。它們一出港口就分散開來,每一條駛向期望能找到魚的那片海面。老人知道自己要駛向遠方,所以把陸地的氣息拋在後方,划進海洋上清晨的清新氣息中。他划到海裏的某一片水域,看見果囊馬尾藻閃出的磷光,漁夫們把這片水域叫"大井",

因為那裏水深突然達到七百英尋[24]，海流衝擊在海底深淵的峭壁上，激起了漩渦，各種魚類都聚集在那裏。這裏集中着海蝦和可作魚餌的小魚，在那些深不可測的水底洞穴裏，有時還有成羣的柔魚，牠們在夜間浮到緊靠海面的地方，所有在那裏漫遊的魚類都拿牠們當食物。

老人在黑暗中感覺到早晨在來臨，他划着划着，聽見飛魚出水時的顫抖聲，還有牠們在黑暗中凌空飛走時挺直的翅膀所發出的噝噝聲。他非常喜愛飛魚，因為牠們是他在海洋上的主要朋友。他替那些鳥傷心，尤其是那些柔弱的黑色小燕鷗，牠們始終在飛翔，在找食，但幾乎從沒找到過，於是他想，小鳥的生活過得比我們的還要艱難，除了那些猛禽和強有力的大鳥。既然海洋這樣殘暴，為甚麼像這些海燕那樣的鳥，生來就如此柔弱和纖巧？海洋是仁慈並十分美麗的。然而她能變得這樣殘暴，又來得這樣突然，而這些飛翔的鳥，從空中落下覓食，發出細微的哀鳴，卻生來就柔弱得不適宜在海上生活。

他每想到海洋，老是稱她為 la mar，這是人們對海洋抱着好感時用西班牙語對她的稱呼。有時候，對海洋抱着好感的人們也說她的壞話，不過說起來總是拿她當女性看待的。[25] 有些較年輕的漁夫，用浮標當釣索上的浮子，並且在把鯊魚肝賣了好多錢後置備了汽艇，都把海洋叫 el mar，這是表示男性的說法。他們提起她時，拿她當作一個競爭者或一個去處，甚至當作一個敵人。可是這老人總是拿海洋當作女性，她給人或者不願給人莫大的恩惠，如果她做出了任性或缺德的事來，那是因為她身不由己。月亮對她起着影響，如同對一個女人那樣，他想。

他平穩地划着，對他説來並不費勁，因為他好好保持在自己的最高速度以內，而且除了水流偶爾打個旋以外，海面是平坦無浪的。他正讓海流幫他做了三份之一的工作，這時天漸漸亮了，他發現自己已經划到比預期此刻能到達的地方更遠了。

我在這海底的深淵上轉遊了一個禮拜，可是一無作為，他想。今天，我要找到那些鰹魚和長鰭金槍魚羣在甚麼地方，説不定會有條大魚跟牠們在一起。

不等天色大亮，他就放出了一個個魚餌，讓船隨着海流漂去。有個魚餌下沉到四十英尋的深處。第二個在七十五英尋的深處，第三個和第四個分別在一百英尋和一百二十五英尋深的藍色海水中。每個由新鮮沙甸魚做的魚餌都是頭朝下的，釣鈎的鈎身穿進小魚的身子，給紮好，縫牢，因此釣鈎的所有突出部份，彎鈎和尖端，都給包在魚肉裏。每條沙甸魚都用釣鈎穿過雙眼，這樣魚的身子在突出的鋼鈎上構成了半個環形。釣鈎上就沒有哪一部份不會叫一條大魚覺得噴香而美味的。

男孩給了他兩條新鮮的小金槍魚，或者叫做長鰭金槍魚，牠們正像鉛錘般掛在那兩根最深的釣索上，在另外兩根上，他掛上了一條藍色海水魚和一條黃色金銀魚，它們已被使用過，但依然完好，而且還有出色的沙甸魚給它們添上香味和吸引力。每根釣索都像一支大鉛筆那麼粗，一端給纏在一根青皮釣竿上，這樣，只要魚在魚餌上一拉或一碰，就能使釣竿下垂，而每根釣索有兩個四十英尋長的卷，它們可以牢繫在其他備用的卷上，這一來，如果用得着的話，一條魚可以拉出三百多英尋長的釣索。

這時老人察看着那三根挑出在小帆船一邊的釣竿有沒有動

靜，一邊緩緩地划着，使釣索保持上下筆直，停留在適當的水底深處。天相當亮了，太陽隨時會升起來。

淡淡的太陽從海上升起，老人看見其他的船隻，低低地挨着水面，離海岸不遠，和海流的方向垂直地展開着。跟着太陽越發明亮了，耀眼的陽光射在水面上，隨後太陽從地平線上完全升起，平坦的海面把陽光反射到他眼睛裏，使眼睛劇烈地刺痛，因此他不朝太陽看，顧自划着。他俯視水中，注視着那幾根一直下垂到黑黑的深水裏的釣索。他把釣索垂得比任何人更直，這樣，在黑黑的灣流深處的幾個不同的深度，都會有一個魚餌，剛好在他想要它在的地方，等待着在那裏游動的魚來吃。別的漁夫讓釣索隨着海流漂去，有時候釣索在六十英尋的深處，他們卻自以為在一百英尋的深處呢。

不過，他想，我總是把它們精確地放在適當的地方的。只是我再也沒有好運了。可是誰說得準呢？說不定今天就轉運。每一天都是一個新的日子。走運當然更好。不過我情願做到分毫不差。這樣，運氣來的時候，你就有所準備了。

兩小時過去了，太陽如今相應地升得更高了，他朝東望時不再感到那麼刺眼了。眼前只看得見三條船，它們顯得特別低矮，遠在近岸的海面上。

我這一輩子，初升的太陽老是刺痛我的眼睛，他想。然而眼睛還是好好的。傍晚時分，我可以直望着太陽，不會有眼前發黑的感覺。陽光的力量在傍晚也要強一些。不過在早上它叫人感到眼痛。

就在這時，他看見一隻黑色的長翅膀軍艦鳥，在他前方的天空中盤旋飛翔。牠慢地斜着後掠的雙翅俯衝，然後又盤旋起來。

"牠捉住甚麼東西了，"老人説出聲來。"牠不光是找找罷了。"

他慢慢划着，直朝那隻鳥盤旋的地方划去。他並不着急，讓那些釣索保持着上下筆直的位置。不過他還是挨近了一點海流，這樣，他依然在用正確的方式捕魚，儘管他的速度要比他不打算利用鳥來指路時來得快。

軍艦鳥在空中飛得高些了，又盤旋起來，雙翅紋絲不動。牠隨即猛然俯衝下來，老人看見飛魚從海裏躍出，在海面上拼命地掠去。

"海豚，"老人説出聲來。"大海豚。"

他把雙槳從槳架上取下，從船頭下面拿出一根細釣絲。釣絲上繫着一段鐵絲導線和一隻中號釣鈎，他拿一條沙甸魚掛在上面。他把釣絲從船舷放下水去，將上端緊緊在船梢一隻拳頭螺栓上。跟着他在另一根釣絲上鈎上了魚餌，把它盤繞着攔在船頭的陰影裏。他又划起船來，注視着那隻此刻正在水面上低低地飛掠的長翅膀黑鳥。

他看着看着，那鳥又朝下衝，為了俯衝，把翅膀朝後掠，然後突然展開，追蹤着飛魚，可是沒有成效。老人看見那些大海豚跟隨在脫逃的魚後面，把海面弄得微微隆起。海豚在飛掠的魚下面破水而行，只等飛魚一掉下，就飛快地鑽進水裏。這羣海豚真大啊，他想。牠們分佈得很廣，飛魚很少脫逃的機會。那隻鳥可沒有成功的機會。飛魚對牠來説太大了，而且又飛得太快。

他看着飛魚一再地從海裏冒出來，看着那隻鳥毫無效果的行動。那羣魚從我附近逃走啦，他想。牠們逃得太快，游得太遠啦。不過說不定我能捉住一條掉隊的，說不定我想要的大魚就在牠們周圍轉遊着。我的大魚總該在某處地方啊。

　　陸地上空的雲塊這時像山岡般聳立着，海岸只剩下一長條綠色的線，背後是些灰青色的小山。海水此刻呈深藍色，深得簡直發紫了。他仔細俯視着海水，只見深藍色的水中穿梭地閃出點點紅色的浮游生物，陽光這時在水中變幻出奇異的光彩。他注視着那幾根釣索，看見它們一直朝下沒入水中看不見的地方，他很高興看到這麼多浮游生物，因為這說明有魚。太陽此刻升得更高了，陽光在水中變幻出奇異的光彩，說明天氣晴朗，陸地上空的雲塊的形狀也說明了這一點。可是那隻鳥這時幾乎看不見了，水面上沒甚麼東西，只有幾攤被太陽曬得發白的黃色馬尾藻和一隻緊靠着船舷浮動的僧帽水母，牠那膠質的浮囊呈紫色，具有一定的外形，閃現出虹彩。牠倒向一邊，然後豎直了身子。牠像個大氣泡般高高興興地浮動着，那些厲害的紫色長觸鬚在水中拖在身後，長達一碼。

　　"水母，"老人說。"你這婊子。"

　　他從坐着輕輕蕩槳的地方低頭朝水中望去，看見一些顏色跟拖在水中的那些觸鬚一樣的小魚，牠們在觸鬚和觸鬚之間，以及浮囊在浮動時所投下的一小攤陰影中游着。牠們對牠的毒素是不受影響的。可是人就不同了，當老人把一條魚拉回船來時，有些觸鬚會纏在釣索上，紫色的黏液附在上面，他的胳臂和手上就會出現傷痕和瘡腫，就像被毒漆樹或櫟葉毒漆樹感染時一樣。但是這水母的毒素發作得更快，使人痛得像被鞭子抽一般。

這些閃着虹彩的大氣泡很美。然而牠們正是海裏最欺詐成性的生物，所以老人樂意看到大海龜把牠們吃掉。海龜發現了牠們，就從正面向牠們進逼，然後閉上眼睛，這樣，從頭到尾完全被硬殼所保護，就把水母連同觸鬚一併吃掉。老人喜歡觀看海龜把牠們吃掉，喜歡在風暴過後在海灘上遇上牠們，喜歡聽到自己用長着老繭的硬腳掌踩在上面時牠們啪地爆裂的聲音。

他喜歡綠色的海龜和玳瑁，牠們形態優美，游水迅速，價值很高，他還對那又大又笨的蠵龜抱着不懷惡意的輕蔑，牠們的甲殼是黃色的，做愛的方式是奇特的，高高興興地吞食僧帽水母時閉上了眼睛。

他對海龜並不抱着神秘的看法，儘管曾多年乘小船去捕海龜。他替所有的海龜傷心，甚至包括那些跟小帆船一樣長、重達一噸的大梭龜。人們大都對海龜殘酷無情，因為一隻海龜給剖開、殺死之後，它的心臟還要跳動好幾個鐘頭。然而老人想，我也有這樣一顆心臟，我的手腳也跟牠們的一樣。他吃白色的海龜蛋，為了使身子長力氣。他在五月份連吃了整整一個月，使自己到九、十月份能身強力壯，去捕真正的大魚。

他每天還從不少漁夫存放工具的棚屋中一隻大圓桶裏舀一杯鯊魚肝油喝。這桶就放在那裏，想喝的漁夫都可以去喝。大多數漁夫厭惡這種油的味道。但是也並不比摸黑早起更叫人難受，而且它對防治一切傷風流感都非常有效，對眼睛也有好處。

老人此刻抬眼望去，看見那隻鳥又在盤旋了。

"牠找到魚啦，"他說出聲來。這時沒有一條飛魚衝出海面，也沒有小魚紛紛四處逃竄。然而老人望着望着，只見一條小金槍魚躍到空中，一個轉身，頭朝下掉進水裏。這條金槍魚在陽光中閃出銀白色的光，等牠回到了水裏，又有一條條金槍魚躍出水面，牠們是朝四面八方跳的，跳得很遠，捕食小魚，攪得海水翻騰起來。牠們正繞着小魚轉，驅趕着小魚。

要不是牠們游得這麼快，我倒要趕到牠們中間去，老人想，他便注視着這羣魚把水攪得泛白，還有那隻鳥，這時正俯衝下來，扎進在驚慌中被迫浮上海面的小魚羣。

"這隻鳥真是個大幫手，"老人説。就在這時，船梢那根細釣絲在他腳下繃緊了，原來他在腳上繞了一圈，於是他放下雙槳，緊緊抓住細釣絲，動手往回拉，感到那小金槍魚在釣絲上顫抖着，有點拉力。他越往回拉，釣絲就越是顫抖，他看見水裏藍色的魚背和金色的兩側，然後把釣絲呼的一甩，使魚越過船舷，掉在船中。魚躺在船梢的陽光裏，身子結實，形狀像顆子彈，一雙癡呆的大眼睛直瞪着，動作乾淨利落的尾巴敏捷、發抖地拍打着船板，砰砰有聲，逐漸耗盡了力氣。老人出於好意，猛擊了一下牠的頭，一腳把牠那還在抖動的身子踢到船梢背陰的地方。

"長鰭金槍魚，"他説出聲來。"拿來釣大魚倒挺好。牠該有十磅重吧。"

他記不起自己甚麼時候開始在獨自一人的時候自言自語了。往年他獨自一人時曾唱歌，有時候在夜裏唱，那是在小漁船或捕海龜的小艇上值班掌舵時的事。他大概是在那男孩走了，才在獨自一人時開始自言自語的。不過他記不清了。他跟男孩一起捕魚時，他們一般只在有必要時才説話。他們在夜間説話，或者，在碰到壞天氣，被暴風雨困在海上的時候説。沒有必要就不在海上説話，被認為是種好規矩，老人一向認為的確如此，才始終遵守。可是這段時間他把心裏想説的話説出聲來有好幾次了，因為沒有旁人會受到他説話的干擾。

"要是別人聽到我在自言自語，會當我發瘋了，"他説出聲來。"不過既然我沒有發瘋，我就不管，還是要説。有錢人在船上有收音機跟他們説話，還把棒球賽的消息告訴他們。"

現在可不是思量棒球賽的時刻，他想。現在只應該思量一件事。就是我生來要做的那件事。那個魚羣周圍很可能有一條大的，他想。我只捉住了正在吃小魚的金槍魚羣中一條失散的。可是牠們正游向遠方，游得很快。今天凡是在海面上露面的都游得很快，向着東北方向。難道一天的這個時辰該是如此嗎？或者，這是甚麼我不懂得的天氣徵兆？

他現在已看不見海岸的那一道綠色了，只看得見那些青山的彷彿積着白雪的山峯，以及山峯上空像是高聳的雪山般的雲塊。海水顏色深極了，陽光在海水中幻成彩虹七色。那數不清的斑斑點點的浮游生物，由於此刻太陽升到了頭頂上空，都看不見了，現在老人看得見的僅僅是藍色海水深處的巨大的七色光帶，還有他那幾根筆直垂在有一英里深的水中的釣索。

漁夫們把所有這種魚都叫金槍魚，只有等到把牠們出售或者拿來換魚餌時，才分別叫牠們各自的專門名字。這時牠們又沉下海去了。陽光此刻很熱，老人感到脖頸上熱辣辣的，划着划着，覺得汗水一滴滴地從背上往下淌。

我大可隨波逐流，他想，睡一陣，預先把釣索在腳趾上繞上一圈，有動靜時可以把我弄醒。不過今天是第八十五天，我該一整天好好釣魚。

就在這時，他凝視着釣索，看見其中有一根挑出在水面上的綠色釣竿突然往水中一沉。

"來啦，"他説。"來啦，"他説着收起雙槳，一點也沒碰上船舷。他伸手去拉釣索，把它輕輕地夾在右手大拇指和食指之間。他感到釣索並不抽緊，也沒甚麼力道，就輕鬆地握着。跟着它又動了一下。這次是試探性的一拉，拉得既不緊又不重，他就完全明白這是怎麼回事了。在一百英尋的深處有條大馬林魚正在吃包住鈎尖和鈎身的沙甸魚，這個手工鍛製的釣鈎是從一條小金槍魚的頭部穿出來的。

老人輕巧地攥着釣索，用左手把它從竿子上輕輕解下。他這時可以讓它穿過他手指間滑動，不會讓魚感到一點牽引力。

在離岸這麼遠的地方，牠長到這個月份，一定挺大了，他想。吃魚餌吧，魚啊。吃吧。請你吃吧。這些魚餌多新鮮，而你哪，待在這六百英尺的深處，在這漆黑的冷水裏。在黑暗裏再繞個彎子，拐回來把它們吃了吧。

他感到微弱而輕巧地一拉，跟着較猛烈地一拉，這時準是有條沙甸魚的頭很難從釣鈎上給扯下來。然後沒有一絲動靜了。

"來吧，"老人説出聲來。"再繞個彎子吧。聞聞這些魚餌。它們不是挺鮮美嗎？趁新鮮把它們吃了，等下還有那條金槍魚呢。又結實，又涼快，又鮮美。別怕難為情，魚。把它們吃了吧。"

他把釣索夾在大拇指和食指之間等待着。同時盯着它和其他那幾根釣索，因為這魚可能已游到了高一點或低一點的地方去了。跟着又是那麼輕巧地一拉。

"牠會咬餌的，"老人說出聲來。"求天主讓牠咬餌吧。"

然而牠沒有咬餌。牠游走了，老人沒感到有任何動靜。

"牠不可能游走的，"他說。"天知道牠是不可能游走的。牠正在繞彎子呢。也許牠以前上過鈎，還有點記得。"

跟着他感到釣索輕輕地動了一下，於是他高興了。

"牠剛才不過是在轉身，"他說。"牠會咬餌的。"

感到這輕微的一拉，他很高興，接着感到有些猛拉的感覺，很有力量，叫人難以相信。這是魚本身的重量造成的，他就鬆手讓釣索朝下、朝下、朝下溜，從那兩卷備用釣索中的一卷上放出釣索。它從老人指間輕輕溜下去的時候，他依舊感到很大的力道，儘管他的大拇指和食指施加的壓力簡直小得覺察不到。

"多厲害的魚啊，"他說。"牠正把魚餌斜叼在嘴裏，帶着牠游開去。"

牠就會掉過頭來把餌吞下去的，他想。他沒有把這句話說出聲來，因為他知道，一件好事如果說破了，也許就不會發生了。他知道這條魚有多大，他想像到牠嘴裏橫銜着金槍魚，正在黑暗中遊蕩。這時他覺得牠停止不動了，可是力道還是沒變。跟着力道越來越重了，他就再放出一點釣索。他一時加強了大拇指和食指上的壓力，於是釣索上的力道增加了，一直傳到水中深處。

"牠咬餌啦，"他說。"現在我來讓牠好好地吃一頓。"

他讓釣索在指間朝下溜，同時朝下伸出左手，把兩卷備用釣索的一端緊繫在旁邊那根釣索的兩卷備用釣索上。他如今準備好了。他現在除了正在使用的那釣索卷，還有三個四十英尋長的卷可供備用。

"再吃一些吧，"他説。"好好地吃吧。"

吃了吧，這樣可以讓釣鈎的尖端扎進你的心臟，把你弄死，他想。輕鬆愉快地浮上來吧，讓我把魚叉刺進你的身子。行了。你準備好了？你進餐的時間夠長了吧？

"起!"他説出聲來，用雙手使勁猛拉釣索，收進了一碼，然後連連猛拉，使出胳膊上的全部力氣，拿身子的重量作為支撐，揮動雙臂，輪換地把釣索往回拉。

甚麼用也沒有。那魚只顧慢慢地游開去，老人無法把牠往上拉一英寸。他這釣索很結實，是製作來釣大魚的，他把它套在背上猛拉，釣索給繃得太緊，上面竟蹦出水珠來。隨後它在水裏漸漸發出一陣嗖嗖聲，但他依舊攥着它，在座板上死勁撐住了自己的身子，仰起上半身來抵消魚的拉力。船慢慢地向西北方向駛去。

大魚一刻不停地游着，魚和船在平靜的水面上慢慢地行進。另外那幾個魚餌還在水裏，沒有動靜，用不着應付。

"但願那男孩在這裏就好了，"老人説出聲來。"我正被一條魚拖着走，成了一根繫縴繩的短柱啦。我可以把釣索繫在船舷上。不過這一來那魚會把它扯斷的。我得拼命牽住牠，必要的時候給牠放出釣索。謝謝老天，牠還在朝前游，沒有朝下沉。"

我不知道如果牠決意朝下沉，我該怎麼辦？我不知道如果牠潛入海底，死在那裏，我該怎麼辦？可是我必須做些甚麼。我能做的事情有好多呢。

他攥住了勒在背脊上的釣索，緊盯着它直往水中斜去，而小帆船正不停地朝西北方駛去。

這樣能叫牠送命，老人想。牠不能一直這樣做。然而過了四個鐘頭，那魚照樣拖着這條小帆船，不停地向大海游去，而老人依然緊緊攙着勒在背脊上的釣索。

"我是中午把牠釣上的，"他說。"可我始終還沒見過牠。"

他在釣上這魚以前，早把草帽拉下，緊扣在腦門上，這時勒得他的前額好痛。他還覺得口渴，就雙膝跪下，小心不讓扯動釣索，盡量朝船頭爬去，伸手去取水瓶。他打開瓶蓋，喝了一點。然後靠在船頭上休息。他坐在從桅座上拔下的繞着帆的桅桿上，竭力不去想甚麼，只顧熬下去。

隨後他回頭一望，陸地已沒有一絲蹤影了。這沒有關係，他想。我總能憑着哈瓦那的燈火回港的。太陽下去還有兩個鐘頭，也許不到那時魚就會浮上來。如果牠不上來，也許會隨着月出浮上來。如果牠不這樣做，也許會隨着日出浮上來。我手腳沒有抽筋，我感到身強力壯。是牠的嘴給釣住了啊。不過拉力這樣大，該是條多大的魚啊。牠的嘴準是死死地咬住了那鋼絲釣鈎。但願能看到牠。但願能知道我這對手是甚麼樣子的，哪怕只看一眼也好。

老人憑着觀察天上的星斗，看出那魚那一夜始終沒有改變牠的路線和方向。太陽下去後，天氣轉涼了，老人的背脊、胳膊和衰老的腿上的汗水都乾了，感到發冷。白天裏，他曾把蓋在魚餌匣上的蔴袋取下，攤在陽光裏曬乾。太陽下去後，他把蔴袋繫在脖子上，讓它披在背上，並且小心地把它塞在如今正掛在肩上的釣索下面。有蔴袋墊着釣索，他發現可以彎身向前靠在船頭上，這樣簡直可說很舒服了。這姿勢實在只能說是多少叫人好受一點，可是他自以為簡直可說很舒服了。

我拿牠一點沒辦法，牠也拿我一點沒辦法，他想。只要牠一直這樣下去，就是如此。

他有一次站起身來，隔着船舷撒尿，然後抬眼望着星斗，核對他的航向。釣索從他肩上一直鑽進水裏，看來像一道磷光。魚和船此刻行動放慢了。哈瓦那的燈火也不大輝煌，他於是明白，海流準是在把他們雙方帶向東方。如果我就此看不見哈瓦那炫目的燈光，我們一定是到了更東的地方，他想。因為，如果這魚的路線沒有改變，我準會好幾個鐘頭看得見燈光。不知今天的棒球大聯賽結果如何，他想。做這一行有個收音機才美哪。接着他想，老是惦記着這玩意。想想你正在做的事情吧。你哪能做蠢事啊。

然後他說出聲來，"但願男孩在就好了。可以幫幫我，讓他見識見識這種光景。"

誰也不該上了年紀後獨自一人，他想。不過這也是避免不了的。為了保養體力，我一定要記住趁金槍魚沒壞時就吃。記住了，哪怕你只想吃一點點，也必須在早上吃。記住了，他對自己說。

夜間，兩條鼠海豚游到小船邊來，他聽見牠們翻騰和噴水的聲音。他能辨別出那雄的發出的喧鬧的噴水聲和那雌的發出的喘息般的噴水聲。

"牠們很友愛，"他說。"牠們嬉耍，打鬧，相親相愛。牠們是我們的兄弟，就像飛魚一樣。"

跟着他憐憫起這條被他釣住的大魚來了。牠真出色，真奇特，而且有誰知道牠年齡多大呢，他想。我從沒釣到過這樣強大的魚，也沒見過行動這樣奇特的魚。也許牠太機靈，不願跳出水來。牠原可以跳出水來，或者來個猛衝，把我搞垮。不過，也許牠曾上鈎過好多次，所以知道應該如何搏鬥。牠哪會知道牠的對手只有一個人，而且是個老頭。不過牠是條多大的魚啊，如果魚肉良好，在市場上能賣多大一筆錢啊。牠咬起餌來像條雄魚，拉起釣索來也像雄魚，搏鬥起來一點也不驚慌。不知道牠有沒有甚麼打算，還是跟我一樣，不顧死活？

他想起有一次釣到了一對大馬林魚中的一條。雄魚總是讓雌的先吃，那條上了鈎的正是雌魚，牠發了狂，驚慌失措而絕望地掙扎着，不久就筋疲力盡了，那條雄魚始終待在牠身邊，在釣索下竄來竄去，陪着牠在水面上一起打轉。這雄魚離釣索好近，老人生怕牠會用尾巴把釣索割斷，這尾巴像大鐮刀般鋒利，大小和形狀都和大鐮刀差不多。老人用魚鈎把雌魚鈎上來，用棍子揍牠，握住了那邊緣如砂紙似的輕劍般的長嘴，連連朝牠頭頂打去，直打得牠的顏色變成和鏡子背面的顏色差不多，然後由男孩幫忙，把牠拖上船來，這期間，那雄魚一直待在船舷邊。隨後，當老人忙着解下釣索、準備好去拿起魚叉時，雄魚在船邊高高地跳到空中，看看雌魚在哪裏，然後鑽進深水，牠那淡紫色的翅膀，實際上是牠的胸鰭，大大地張開來，於是牠身上所有的淡紫色寬條紋都露出來了。牠是美麗的，老人想起，而牠始終留在那裏不走。

牠們這情景是我看到的最傷心的了，老人想。男孩也很傷心，因此我們請求這條雌魚原諒，馬上把牠宰了。

"但願男孩在這裏就好了，"他說出聲來，把身子靠在船頭的邊緣已被磨圓的木板上，通過勒在肩上的釣索，感到大魚的力量，而牠正朝着牠所選擇的方向穩穩地游去。

我一旦欺騙了牠，牠便不得不作出選擇了，老人想。

牠選擇的是留在黑暗的深水裏，遠遠地避開一切圈套、羅網和詭計。我選擇的是趕到誰也沒到過的地方去找牠。到世界上沒人去過的地方。如今我跟牠給拴在一起了，從中午起就是如此。而且我和牠都沒有人來幫忙。

也許我不該當漁夫，他想。然而我生來該做這一行。我一定要記住，天亮後就吃那條金槍魚。

離天亮還有點時間，有甚麼東西咬住了他背後的一個魚餌。他聽見釣竿啪地折斷了，於是那根釣索越過船舷朝外直溜，他摸黑拔出鞘中的刀子，用左肩承擔起大魚所有的拉力，身子朝後靠，把木船舷上的釣索割斷。然後把另一根離他最近的釣索也割斷了，摸黑把這兩個備用的釣索卷的斷頭繫在一起。他用一隻手熟練地操作着，在牢牢地打結時，一隻腳踩住了釣索卷，免得移動。他現在有六卷備用釣索了。他剛才割斷的那兩根有魚餌的釣索各有兩卷備用釣索，加上被大魚咬住魚餌的那根上的兩卷，它們全都接在一起了。

等天亮了，他想，我一定要回到那根把魚餌放在水下四十英尋深處的釣索邊，把它也割斷了，連結在那些備用釣索卷上。我將丟掉兩百英尋出色的加泰羅尼亞[26]釣索，還有釣鈎和導線。這些都是能再置備的。萬一釣上了別的魚，把這條大魚倒搞丟了，那該去找甚麼魚來替代呢？我不知道剛才咬餌的是甚麼魚。很可能是條大馬林魚，或者劍魚，或者鯊魚。我根本來不及琢磨。我不得不趕快把牠擺脫掉。

他說出聲來："但願那男孩在就好了。"

可是男孩並不在這裏，他想。你只有你自己一個人，你還是回到最末的那根釣索邊，不管天黑不黑，把它割斷了，繫上那兩卷備用釣索。

他就這樣做了。摸黑做事很困難，有一次，那條大魚掀動了一下，把他拖倒在地，臉朝下，眼睛下給劃了一道口子。鮮血從他臉頰上淌下來。但還沒流到下巴上就凝固、乾掉，於是他挪動身子回到船頭，靠在木船舷上歇息。他拉好蔴袋，把釣索小心地挪到肩上另一個地方，用肩膀把它固定住，握住了小心地試試那魚拉扯的力道，然後伸手到水裏測度小船航行的速度。

不知道這魚為甚麼剛才突然搖晃了一下，他想。一定是釣索在牠高高隆起的背脊上滑動了一下。牠的背脊當然痛得及不上我的。然而不管牠力氣多大，總不能永遠拖着這條小帆船跑吧。現在凡是會惹出亂子來的東西都除掉了，我卻還有好多備用的釣索；一個人還能有甚麼要求呢。

"魚啊，"他輕輕地說出聲來，"我要跟你奉陪到死。"

依我看，牠也要跟我奉陪到死的，老人想，於是他等待着天明。現在正當破曉前的時分，天氣很冷，他把身子緊貼着木船舷來取暖。牠能熬多久，我也能熬多久，他想。天色微明中，釣索伸展着，朝下通到水中。小船平穩地移動着，初升的太陽一露邊，陽光直射在老人的右肩上。

"牠在朝北走啊，"老人說。海流會把我們遠遠地向東方送去，他想。但願牠會隨着海流拐彎。這樣可以說明牠越來越疲乏了。

等太陽升得更高了，老人發覺這魚並不越來越疲乏。只有一個有利的徵兆。釣索的斜度說明牠正在較淺的地方游着。這不一定表示牠會躍出水來。但牠也許會這樣做。

"天主啊，叫牠跳躍吧，"老人說。"我的釣索夠長，可以對付牠。"

也許我把釣索稍微拉緊一點，讓牠覺得痛，牠就會跳躍起來，他想。既然是白天了，就讓牠跳躍吧，這樣牠會把沿着背脊的那些液囊裝滿了空氣，就沒法沉到海底去死了。

他動手拉緊釣索，可是自從釣上這條魚以來，釣索已經繃緊到快要繃斷的地步，他就向後仰着身子來拉，感到它硬硬的，就知道沒法拉得更緊了。我千萬不能突然一拉，他想。每猛拉一次，會把釣鈎劃出的口子弄得更寬些，等牠當真跳躍起來，牠也許就會把釣鈎甩掉。反正太陽出了，我覺得好過些，這一次我不用盯着太陽看了。

釣索上黏着黃色的海藻，可是老人知道這只會給魚增加一些拉力，所以很高興。正是這種黃色的果囊馬尾藻在夜間發出那麼強的磷光。

"魚啊，"他說，"我愛你，非常尊敬你。不過今天我得把你殺死。"

但願如此，他想。

一隻小鳥從北方朝小帆船飛來。那是隻鳴禽，在水面上飛得很低。老人看出牠非常疲乏了。

那隻鳥飛到船梢上，在那裏歇一口氣。然後牠繞着老人的頭飛了一圈，落在那根釣索上，在那裏牠覺得比較舒服。

"你多大了？"老人問那隻鳥。"你這是第一次出門吧？"

他説話的時候，那小鳥望着他。牠太疲乏了，竟沒有細看這釣索，就用小巧的雙腳緊抓住了釣索，在上面搖啊晃的。

"這釣索很穩當，"老人對牠説。"太穩當啦。夜裏風息全無，你怎麼會這樣疲乏啊。這些鳥都怎麼啦？"

因為有老鷹，他想，飛到海上來追捕牠們。但是這話他沒跟這鳥説，反正牠也不懂他的話，而且很快就會知道老鷹的厲害。

"好好休息吧，小鳥，"他説。"然後飛到空中去碰碰運氣，像任何人或者鳥或者魚那樣。"

他靠説話來鼓勁，因為他的背脊在夜裏變得僵直，現在真痛得厲害。

"樂意的話就住在我家吧，小鳥，"他説。"很抱歉，我不能趁現在颳起小風的時候，扯起帆來把你帶回去。可是我總算有個朋友在一起了。"

就在這時，那魚陡地一歪，把老人拖倒在船頭上，要不是他撐住了身子，放出一段釣索，早把他拖到海裏去了。

釣索突然一抽時，小鳥飛走了，老人竟沒有看到牠飛走。他用右手小心地摸摸釣索，發現手上正在淌血。

"這麼説這魚給甚麼東西弄傷了，"他説出聲來，把釣索往回拉，看能不能叫魚轉回來。但是拉到快繃斷的時候，他就握穩了釣索，身子朝後倒，來抵消釣索上的那股拉力。

"你現在覺得痛了吧，魚，"他説。"老實説，我也是如此啊。"

他掉頭尋找那隻小鳥，因為很樂意有牠來作伴。可是牠飛走了。

你沒有待多久啊，老人想。但是你去的地方風浪較大，要飛到了岸上才平安。我怎麼會讓那魚突然一拉，割破了手？我一定是越來越笨了。或者，也許是因為只顧望着那隻小鳥，想着牠的事。現在我要關心自己的事情，過後得把那金槍魚吃下，這樣才不致沒力氣。

"但願男孩在這裏，我手邊有點鹽，"他說出聲來。

他把沉重的釣索挪到左肩上，小心地跪下，在海水裏洗手，把手在水裏浸了一分多鐘，注視着血液在水中漂開去，而那平穩地流着的海水隨着船的移動在他手上拍打着。

"牠游得慢多了，"他說。

老人巴不得讓他的手在這鹽水中多浸一會，但害怕那魚又陡地一歪，於是站起身，打點起精神，舉起那隻手，朝着太陽。只不過被釣索勒了一下，割破了皮肉而已。然而這正是手上最有用的地方。他知道需要這雙手來把這件事做到底，不喜歡還沒動手就讓手給割破。

"現在，"等手曬乾了，他說，"我該吃小金槍魚了。我可以用魚鈎把它鈎過來，在這裏舒舒服服地吃。"

他跪下來，用魚鈎在船梢下找到了那條金槍魚，小心不讓它碰着那幾卷釣索，把它鈎到自己身邊來。他又用左肩挎住了釣索，把左手和胳臂撐在座板上，從魚鈎上取下金槍魚，再把魚鈎放回原處。他把一膝壓在魚身上，從它的脖頸豎割到尾部，割下一條條深紅色的魚肉。這些肉條的斷面是楔形的，他從脊骨邊開始割，直割到肚子邊。他割下了六條，把它們攤在船頭的木板上，在褲子上擦擦刀子，拎起魚尾巴，把魚骨扔在海裏。

"我想我是吃不下一整條的，"他說，用刀子把一條魚肉一切為二。他感到那釣索一直緊拉着，弄得他的左手抽起筋來。這左手緊緊握住了粗釣索，他厭惡地朝它看着。

"這算甚麼手啊，"他說。"隨你去抽筋吧。變成一隻鳥爪吧。對你可不會有好處。"

快點，他想，望着斜向黑暗的深水裏的釣索。快把它吃了，會使手有力氣的。不能怪這隻手不好，因為你跟這魚已經打了好幾個鐘頭的交道啦。不過你是能跟牠周旋到底的。馬上把這小金槍魚吃了。

他拿起半條魚肉，放在嘴裏，慢慢地咀嚼。倒並不難吃。

好好咀嚼，他想，把汁水都嚥下去。如果加上一點酸橙或者檸檬或者鹽，味道可不會壞。

"感覺怎麼樣，手啊？"他問那隻抽筋的手，它僵直得幾乎跟死屍一般。"我要為了你再吃一點。"

他吃着那條他切成兩段的魚肉的另外一半。他細細地咀嚼，然後把魚皮吐出來。

"覺得怎麼樣，手啊？或者，還不到時候，說不上來？"

他拿起一整條魚肉，咀嚼起來。

"這是條壯實而血氣旺盛的魚。"他想。"我運氣好，捉到了牠，而不是條海豚。海豚太甜了。這魚簡直一點也不甜，元氣還都保存着。"

然而最有道理的還是講究實際，他想。但願我有點鹽。我還不知道太陽會不會把剩下的魚肉給曬壞或者曬乾，所以最好把它們都吃了，儘管我並不餓。那魚現在又平靜又安穩。我把這些魚肉統統吃了，就有所準備啦。

"耐心點吧，手啊，"他說。"我這樣吃東西是為了你啊。"

我巴望也能餵那條大魚，他想。牠是我的兄弟。可是我不得不把牠弄死，而且得保持精力來這樣做。他認真地慢慢地把那些楔形的魚肉條全都吃了。

他直起腰來，把手在褲子上擦了擦。

"行了，"他說。"你可以放掉釣索了，手啊，我要單單用右臂來對付牠，直到你不再胡鬧。"他把左腳踩住剛才用左手攢着的粗釣索，身子朝後倒，用背部來承受那股拉力。

"天主幫助我，讓這抽筋快好吧，"他說。"因為我不知道這條魚還要怎麼樣。"

不過牠似乎很鎮靜，他想，而且在按着牠的計劃行動。可是牠的計劃是甚麼，他想。我的又是甚麼？我必須隨機應變，拿我的計劃來對付牠的，因為牠長得這麼大。如果牠跳出水來，我就能弄死牠。但是牠始終留在下面不上來。那我也就要跟牠奉陪到底。

他把那隻抽筋的手在褲子上擦擦，想使手指鬆動鬆動。可是手張不開來。也許隨着太陽出來它能張開，他想。也許等那些養人的生金槍魚肉消化後，它能張開。如果我非靠這隻手不可，我要不惜任何代價把它張開。但是我現在不願硬把它張開。讓它自行張開，自動恢復過來吧。我昨夜畢竟把它使用得過度了，那時候不得不把各條釣索解開，繫在一起。

他眺望着海面，發覺他此刻是多麼孤單。但是他可以看見深色的海水深處的彩虹七色、面前伸展着的釣索和那平靜的海面上奇妙的波動。由於貿易風[27]的吹颳，這時雲塊正在積聚起來，他朝前望去，見到一羣野鴨在水面上飛，在天空的襯托下，身影刻畫得很清楚，然後模糊起來，然後又清楚地刻畫出來，於是他明白，一個人在海上是永遠不會孤單的。

他想到有些人乘小船駛到瞭望不見陸地的地方，會覺得害怕，他明白在天氣會突然變壞的那幾個月裏，他們是有理由害怕的。可是如今正當颳颶風的月份，而在不颳的時候，這些月份正是一年中天氣最佳的時候。

如果將颳起颶風，而你正在海上的話，你總能在好幾天前就看見天上有種種跡象。人們在岸上可看不見，因為他們不知道該找甚麼，他想。陸地上一定也看得見異常的現象，那就是雲的式樣不同。但是眼前不會颳颶風。

他望望天空，看見一團團白色的積雲，形狀像一堆堆可人心意的冰淇淋，而在高高的上空，九月裏的高空襯托出一縷縷羽毛般的卷雲。

"東北風微微吹，"他說。"這天氣對我比對你更有利，魚啊。"

他的左手依然在抽筋，但他正在慢慢地把它張開。

我恨抽筋，他想。這是對自己身體的背叛行為。由於食物中毒而腹瀉或者嘔吐，是在別人面前丟臉。但是抽筋，他想，在西班牙語中叫 calambre，是丟自己的臉，尤其是獨自一個人的時候。

要是那男孩在這裏，他可以給我揉揉胳臂，從前臂一直往下揉，他想。不過這手總會鬆開的。

隨後，他用右手去摸釣索，感到它拉扯着的力道變了，這才看見在水裏的斜度也變了。跟着他俯身朝着釣索，把左手啪地緊按在大腿上，看見傾斜的釣索在慢慢地向上升起。

"牠上來啦，"他説。"手啊，快點。請快點張開。"

釣索慢慢穩穩上升，接着小船前面的海面鼓起來了，那魚出水了。牠不停地往上冒，水從牠身上向兩邊直瀉。牠在陽光裏亮閃閃的，腦袋和背部呈深紫色，兩側的條紋在陽光裏顯得寬闊，帶着淡紫色。牠的長嘴像棒球棒那樣長，逐漸變細，像一把輕劍，牠把全身從頭到尾都露出水面，然後像潛水員般滑溜地又鑽進水去，老人看見牠那大鐮刀般的尾巴沒入水裏，釣索開始往外飛速溜去。

"牠比這小帆船還長兩英尺，"老人説。釣索朝水中溜得既快又穩，説明這魚並沒有受驚。老人設法用雙手拉住釣索，用的力氣剛好不致被魚扯斷。他明白，要是他沒法用穩定的力道使魚慢下來，牠就會把釣索全部拖走，並且綳斷。

牠是條大魚，我一定要制服牠，他想。我一定不能讓牠明白牠有多大的力氣，明白牠如果飛逃的話，能做出甚麼來。我要是牠，現在就要使出渾身的力氣，一直飛逃到甚麼東西綳斷為止。但是感謝天主，牠們沒有我們這些要殺害牠們的人聰明，儘管牠們比我們高尚，更有能耐。

老人見過許多大魚。他見過許多超過一千磅的，而且前半輩子也曾捕到過兩條這麼大的，不過從未一個人捕到過。現在正是獨自一個人，看不見陸地的影子，卻在跟一條比他曾見過、曾聽說過的更大的魚緊拴在一起，而他的左手依舊拳曲着，像緊抓着的鷹爪。

然而它就會復原的，他想。它當然會復原，來幫助我的右手。有三樣東西是兄弟：那條魚和我的兩隻手。這手一定會復原的。真可恥，它竟會抽筋。魚又慢下來了，正用牠慣常的速度游着。

弄不懂牠剛才為甚麼跳出水來，老人想。簡直像是為了讓我看看牠到底有多大。反正我現在是知道了，他想。但願我也能讓牠看看我是個甚麼樣的人。不過這一來牠會看到這隻抽筋的手了。讓牠以為我的男子漢氣概要比我現在所有的更足，我就能做到這一點。但願我就是這條魚，他想，牠正使出所有的力量，而要對付的僅僅是我的意志和我的智力。

他舒舒服服地靠在木船舷上，忍受着襲上身來的痛楚感，那魚仍穩定地游着，小船穿過深色的海水緩緩前進。隨着東方吹來的風，海上起了小浪，到中午時分，老人那抽筋的左手復原了。

“這對你是壞消息，魚啊，”他說，把釣索從披在他肩上的蔴袋上挪了一下位置。

他感到舒服，但還是覺得痛苦，儘管他根本不承認是痛苦。

“我並不篤信宗教，”他說。“但是我願意唸十遍《天主經》和十遍《聖母經》，使我能捕到這條魚，我還許下心願，如果捕到了牠，一定去朝拜科夫萊的聖母。這是我許下的心願。”

他呆板地唸起祈禱文來。有些時候他太倦了，竟背不出祈禱文，他就唸得特別快，使字句能順口唸出來。《聖母經》要比《天主經》容易唸，他想。

“滿被聖寵的瑪利亞，天主與妳同在。妳是女人中有福的，妳兒子耶穌也是有福的。天主聖母瑪利亞，在今天以及在我們臨死的時刻，為我等罪人祈禱吧。阿門。"然後他加上了兩句："萬福童貞聖母，祈求妳叫這魚死去。儘管牠多了不起。"

唸完了祈禱文，他覺得舒坦多了，但依舊像剛才一樣地痛，也許更厲害一點，於是他背靠在船頭的木舷上，機械地活動起左手的手指。

此刻陽光很熱了，儘管微風正在柔和地吹起。

"我還是把挑出在船梢的細釣絲重新裝上釣餌的好，"他説。"如果那魚打算在這裏再過上一夜，我就需要再吃點東西，再説，水瓶裏的水也不多了。我看這裏除了海豚，也捉不到甚麼別的東西。但是，如果趁牠新鮮的時候吃，味道不會差。我希望今夜有條飛魚跳上船來。可惜我沒有燈光來引誘牠。飛魚生吃味道美得很，而且不用把它切成小塊。我現在必須保存所有的精力。天啊，我當初不知道這魚竟這麼大。"

"可是我要把牠宰了，"他説。"不管牠多麼了不起，多麼神氣。"

然而這是不公平的，他想。不過我要讓牠知道人有多少能耐，人能忍受多少磨難。

"我跟那男孩説過，我是個不同尋常的老頭，"他説。"現在是證實這話的時候了。"

他已經證實過上千次了，這算不上甚麼。現在他正要再證實一次。每一次都是重新開始，他這樣做的時候，從來不去想過去。

但願牠睡去，這樣我也能睡去，夢見獅子，他想。為甚麼如今夢中主要只剩下了獅子？別想了，老頭，他對自己説。現在且輕輕地靠着木船舷歇息，甚麼都不要想。牠正忙碌着。你越少忙碌越好。

時間已是下午，船依舊緩慢而穩定地移動着。不過這時東風給船增加了一份阻力，老人隨着不大的海浪緩緩漂流，釣索勒在他背上的感覺變得容易忍受而平和些了。

下午有一次，釣索又升上來了。可是那魚不過是在稍微高一點的海面下繼續游着。太陽曬在老人的左胳臂、左肩和背脊上。所以他知道這魚轉向東北方了。

既然這魚他看見過一次，他就能想像牠在水裏游的樣子，牠那翅膀般的紫色胸鰭大張着，直豎的大尾巴劃破黝黑的海水。不知道牠在那樣深的海裏能看見多少東西，老人想。牠的眼睛真大，馬的眼睛要小得多，但在黑暗裏看得見東西。從前我在黑暗裏能看得很清楚。可不是在烏漆墨黑的地方。不過簡直能像貓一樣看東西。

陽光和他手指不斷的活動，使他抽筋的左手這時完全復原了，他就着手讓它多負擔一點拉力，並且聳聳背上的肌肉，使釣索挪開一點，把痛處換個地方。

"你要是沒覺得累的話，魚啊，"他說出聲來，"那你真是不可思議啦。"

他這時感到非常疲乏，他知道夜色就要降臨，所以竭力想些別的事。他想到棒球的兩大聯賽，就是他用西班牙語所說的 Gran Ligas，他知道紐約市的洋基隊正在迎戰底特律的老虎隊。

這是聯賽的第二天，可我不知道比賽的結果如何，他想。但是我一定要有信心，一定要對得起那了不起的迪馬喬，他即使腳後跟長了骨刺[28]，感到疼痛，也能把一切做得十全十美。骨刺是甚麼玩意？他問自己。西班牙語叫做 un espuela de hueso。我們沒有這玩意。它痛起來跟鬥雞腳上裝的距刺扎進人的腳後跟時一樣厲害嗎？我想我是忍受不了這種痛苦的，也不能像鬥雞那樣，一隻或兩隻眼睛被啄瞎後仍舊戰鬥下去。人跟偉大的鳥獸相比真算不上甚麼。我還是情願做那隻生活在黑暗的深水裏的動物。

"除非有鯊魚來，"他説出聲來。"如果有鯊魚來，願天主憐憫牠和我吧。"

你以為那了不起的迪馬喬能守着一條魚，像我守着這一條一樣長久嗎？他想。我相信他能，而且更長久，因為他年輕力壯。加上他父親當過漁夫。不過骨刺會不會使他痛得太厲害呢？

"我説不上來，"他説出聲來。"我從沒長過骨刺。"

太陽落下去的時候，為了給自己增強信心，他回想起那次在卡薩布蘭卡[29]一家酒店裏，跟那個碼頭上力氣最大的人，從西恩富戈斯[30]來的大個子黑人比手勁的光景。整整一天一夜，他們把手肘擱在桌面一道粉筆線上，胳膊朝上伸直，兩隻手緊握着。雙方都竭力將對方的手使勁朝下壓到桌面上。賭注下了真不少，人們在室內的煤油燈下走出走進，他打量着黑人的胳膊和手，還有這黑人的臉。最初的八小時過後，他們每四小時換一名裁判，好讓裁判輪流睡覺。他和黑人手上的指甲縫裏都滲出血來，他們緊盯着彼此的眼睛，望着對方的手和胳膊，那些打賭的人在屋裏走出走進，坐在靠牆的高腳椅子上旁觀。四壁漆着明亮的藍色，是木製的板壁，幾盞燈把他們的影子投射在牆上。黑人的影子非常大，隨着微風吹動掛燈，這影子在牆上移動着。

一整夜，賭注的賠率來回變換着，人們把朗姆酒送到黑人嘴邊，替他點燃香煙。黑人喝了朗姆酒，拼命使出勁來，老人呢，當時還不是個老人，而是"冠軍"聖地亞哥，有一次他的手被扳下去將近三英寸。然而老人把手扳回來，又成為平手了。他當時確信自己已佔了這黑人的上風，那是個很不錯的黑人，了不起的運動員。天亮時，打賭的人們要求當和局算了，裁判直搖頭，老人卻使出了渾身的力氣，硬是把黑人的手一點點朝下扳，直到擱在桌面上。這場比賽是在一個星期天的早上開始的，直到星期一早上才結束。好多打賭的人要求算是和局，因為他們得上碼頭去做事，把蔴袋裝的蔗糖裝上船，或者上哈瓦那煤行去工作。要不然人人都會要求比賽到底的。但是他反正把它結束了，而且趕在任何人上工之前。

此後好一陣子，人人都叫他"冠軍"，第二年春天又舉行了一場比賽。不過賭注的數目不大，他很容易就贏了，因為他在那第一場比賽中打垮了那個西恩富戈斯來的黑人的自信心。他後來又比賽過幾次，就再也不比了。他認為如果一心想要做到的話，他能夠打敗任何人，他還認為，這對他要用來釣魚的右手有害。他曾嘗試用左手作了幾次練習賽。但是他的左手一向背叛他，不願聽他的吩咐行動，他不信任它。

太陽就會把手好好曬乾的，他想。它不會再抽筋了，除非夜裏太冷。不知道這一夜會發生甚麼事。

一架飛機在他頭上飛過，正循着航線飛向邁阿密，他看着它的影子把成羣的飛魚驚得躍出水面。

"有這麼多的飛魚，這裏該有海豚，"他說，倒身向後靠在釣索上，看能不能把那魚拉過來一點。但是不行，釣索照樣緊繃着，上面抖動着水珠，都快繃斷了。船緩緩地前進，他緊盯着飛機，直到看不見為止。

坐在飛機裏一定感覺很怪，他想。不知道從那麼高的地方朝下望，海是甚麼樣子？要不是飛得太高，他們一定能清楚地看到這條魚。我希望在兩百英尋的高度飛得極慢極慢，從空中看魚。在捕海龜的船上，我待在桅頂橫桁上，即使從那樣的高度也能看到不少東西。從那裏朝下望，海豚的顏色更綠，你能看清牠們身上的條紋和紫色斑點，你可以看見牠們整整一羣在游水。怎麼搞的，凡是在深暗的水流中游得很快的魚都有紫色的背脊，一般還有紫色條紋或斑點？海豚在水裏當然看上去是綠色的，因為牠們實際上是金黃色的。但是當牠們餓得慌，想吃東西的時候，身子兩側就會出現紫色條紋，就像大馬林魚那樣。是因為憤怒，還是游得太快，才使這些條紋顯露出來的呢？

就在天黑之前，老人和船經過好大一片馬尾藻，它在風浪很小的海面上動盪着，彷彿海洋正同甚麼東西在一條黃色的毯子下做愛，這時，他那根細釣絲給一條海豚咬住了。他第一次看見牠是在牠躍出水面的時刻，在最後一線陽光中呈真金色，牠在空中彎起身子，瘋狂地撲打着。牠驚慌得一次次躍出水面，像在做雜技表演，他便慢慢地挪動身子，回到船梢蹲下，用右手和右臂攥住那根粗釣索，用左手把海豚往回拉，每收回一段釣絲，就用光着的左腳踩住。等到這條帶紫色斑點的金光燦爛的魚給拉到了船梢邊，絕望地左右亂竄亂跳時，老人探出身去，把牠拎到船梢上。牠的嘴被釣鈎掛住了，抽搐地動着，急促地連連咬着釣鈎，還用牠那長而扁的身體、尾巴和腦袋拍打着船底，直到他用木棍打了一下牠金光閃亮的腦袋，牠才抖了一下，不動了。

老人把釣鈎從魚嘴裏拔出來，重新鈎上一條沙甸魚作餌，把它甩進海裏。然後他挪動身子慢慢地回到船頭。他洗了左手，在褲腿上擦乾。跟着他把那根粗釣索從右手挪到左手，在海裏洗着右手，同時望着太陽沉到海裏，還望着那根斜入水中的粗釣索。

"那魚還是老樣子，一點也沒變，"他說。但是他注視着海水如何拍打在他手上，發覺船走得顯然慢些了。

"我來把這兩支槳交叉綁在船梢，這樣在夜裏能使那魚慢下來，"他說。"牠能熬夜，我也能。"

最好稍等一會再把這海豚開膛剖肚，這樣可以讓鮮血留在魚肉裏，他想。我可以等一會再這樣做，現在且把槳紮起來，在水裏拖着，增加阻力。這個時候還是讓魚安靜些的好，在日落時分別去過份驚動牠。對所有的魚來說，太陽落下去的時分都是難熬的。

他把手舉起來晾乾了，然後攥住釣索，盡量放鬆身子，聽任自己被拖向前去，身子貼在木船舷上，這樣船承擔的拉力和他自己承擔的一樣大，也許更大些。

我漸漸學會該怎麼做了，他想。反正至少在這一方面是如此。再說，別忘了牠咬餌以來還沒吃過東西，而且牠身子龐大，需要很多的食物。我已經把這整條金槍魚吃了。明天我將吃那條海豚。他把它叫做"黃金魚"。也許我該在把它開膛清腸時吃上一點。它比那條金槍魚要難吃些。不過話得說回來，做甚麼都不容易。

"你覺得怎麼樣，魚啊？"他開口問。"我覺得很好過，我左手已經好轉了，我有可供一夜和一個白天吃的食物。拖着這船吧，魚啊。"

他並不真正覺得好過，因為釣索勒在背上疼痛得幾乎超出了能忍痛的極限，進入了一種使他不放心的麻木狀態。不過比這更糟的事情我也曾碰到過，他想。我一隻手僅僅割破了一點，另一隻手的抽筋已經好了。我的兩條腿都沒有問題。再說，在補給營養方面我也比牠佔優勢。

這時天黑了，因為在九月裏，太陽一落，天馬上就黑下來。他背靠着船頭上給磨損的木船弦，盡量充份休息。第一批星星露面了。他不知道其中有一顆叫 Rigel[31]，但是看到了它，就知道其他星星不久都要露面，他又有這些遙遠的朋友來做伴了。

"這條魚也是我的朋友，"他說出聲來。"我從沒見過或聽說過這樣的魚。不過我必須把牠弄死。我很高興，我們不必去弄死那些星星。"

想想看，如果人必須每天去弄死月亮，那該多糟，他想。月亮會逃走的。不過想想看，如果人必須每天去弄死太陽，那又怎麼樣？我們總算生來是幸運的，他想。

於是他替這條沒東西吃的大魚感到傷心，但是要殺死牠的決心絕對沒有因為替牠傷心而減弱。牠能供多少人吃啊，他想。可是他們配吃牠嗎？不配，當然不配。憑牠的舉止風度和牠的高度尊嚴來看，誰也不配吃牠。

我弄不懂這些事情，他想。可是我們不必去弄死太陽或月亮或星星，倒是好事。在海上過日子，弄死我們自己真正的兄弟，已經讓我們受夠了。

現在，他想，我該考慮考慮那在水裏拖着的障礙物了。這玩意有它的危險，也有它的好處。如果魚使勁地拉，增加阻力的那兩把槳在原處並不鬆動，船不像從前那樣輕的話，我可能會被魚拖走好長的釣索，結果會讓牠跑了。保持船身輕，會延長我們雙方的痛苦，但這是我的安全所在，因為這魚能游得很快，這本領至今尚未使出過。不管出甚麼事，我必須把這海豚開膛剖肚，免得壞掉，並且吃一點以增長力氣。

現在我要再休息一個鐘頭，等我感到魚穩定了下來，才回到船梢去做這事，並決定對策。在這段時間裏，我可以看牠怎樣行動，是否有甚麼變化。把那兩把槳放在那裏是個好計策；不過已經到了該安全行事的時候。這魚依舊很厲害。我見過那釣鈎掛在牠的嘴角，牠把嘴閉得緊緊的。釣鈎的折磨算不上甚麼。飢餓的折磨，加上還得對付牠這不了解的對手，才是天大的麻煩。休息吧，老傢伙，讓牠去做牠的事，等輪到該你做的時候再說。

他自以為已經休息了兩個鐘頭。月亮要等到很晚才爬上來，他沒法判斷時間。實際上他並沒有好好休息，只能說是多少歇了一會。他肩上依舊承受着魚的拉力，不過他把左手按在船頭的舷上，把對抗魚的拉力的任務越來越讓小帆船本身來承擔了。

要是能把釣索拴住，那事情會變得多簡單啊，他想。可是只消魚稍微歪一歪，就能把釣索繃斷。我必須用自己的身子來緩衝這釣索的拉力，隨時準備用雙手放出釣索。

"不過你還沒睡覺呢，老頭，"他說出聲來。"已經熬過了半個白天和一夜，現在又是一個白天，可你一直沒睡覺。你必須想個辦法，趁魚安靜穩定的時候睡上一會。如果你不睡覺，你會搞得腦筋糊塗起來。"

我腦筋夠清醒的，他想。太清醒啦。我跟星星一樣清醒，它們是我的兄弟。不過我還是必須睡覺。它們睡覺，月亮和太陽都睡覺，連海洋有時候也睡覺，那是在某些沒有激浪，平靜無波的日子裏。

可別忘了睡覺，他想。強迫你自己睡覺，想出些簡單而穩妥的辦法來安排那些釣索。現在回到船梢去處理那條海豚吧。如果你一定要睡覺的話，把槳綁起來拖在水裏可就太危險啦。

我不睡覺也能行，他對自己說。不過這太危險啦。

他用雙手雙膝爬回船梢，小心避免突然驚動那條魚。牠也許正是半睡半醒的，他想。可是我不想讓牠休息。必須要牠拖曳着一直到死去。

回到了船梢，他轉身讓左手攥住緊勒在肩上的釣索，用右手從刀鞘中拔出刀子。星星這時很明亮，他清楚地看見那條海豚，就把刀刃扎進牠的頭部，把牠從船梢下拉出來。他用一隻腳踩在魚身上，從肛門朝上，倏地一刀直剖到牠下頜的尖端。然後他放下刀子，用右手掏出內臟，掏個乾淨，把鰓也乾脆拉下。他覺得魚胃在手裏有點重重的、滑滑的，就把它剖開。裏面有兩條小飛魚。牠們還很新鮮、堅實，他把它們並排放下，把內臟和魚鰓從船梢扔進水中。它們沉下去時，在水中拖出一道磷光。海豚是冰冷的，這時在星光裏顯得像痲瘋病患者般灰白，老人用右腳踩住魚頭，剝下魚身上一邊的皮。然後他把魚翻轉過來，剝掉另一邊的皮，把魚身兩邊的肉從頭到尾割下。

他把魚骨悄悄地丟到舷外，注意看它會不會在水裏打轉。但是只看到它慢慢沉下時的磷光。跟着他轉過身來，把兩條飛魚夾在那兩片魚肉中間，把刀子插進刀鞘，慢慢挪動身子，回到船頭。他被釣索上的力道拉得彎了腰，右手拿着魚肉。

回到船頭後，他把兩片魚肉攤在船板上，旁邊擱着飛魚。然後他把勒在肩上的釣索換一個地方，又用左手攥住了釣索，手擱在船舷上。接着他從船舷探出身去，把飛魚在水裏洗洗，留意着水衝擊在他手上有多快。他的手因為剝了魚皮而發出磷光，他仔細察看水流怎樣衝擊他的手。水流並不那麼有力了，當他把手的側面在小帆船船板上擦着的時候，星星點點的磷質漂浮開去，慢慢朝船梢漂去。

"牠越來越累了，要麼就是在休息，"老人說。"現在我來把這海豚全吃了，休息一下，睡一會吧。"

在星光下，在越來越冷的夜色裏，他把一片海豚肉吃了一半，還吃了一條已經挖去了內臟、切掉了腦袋的飛魚。

"海豚煮熟了吃味道才鮮美啊，"他說。"生吃可難吃死了。以後不帶鹽或酸橙，我絕對不再乘船了。"

如果我有頭腦，我會整天不斷把海水潑在船頭上，等它乾了就會有鹽了，他想。不過話得說回來，我是直到太陽快落山時才釣到這條海豚的。但畢竟是準備工作做得不足。然而我把它全細細咀嚼後吃下去了，沒有噁心作嘔。

東方天空中佈滿了雲，他認識的星星一顆顆地不見了。他現在彷彿正駛進一個雲彩的大峽谷，風已經停了。

"三四天內會有壞天氣，"他說。"但是今晚和明天還不要緊。

現在來安排一下，老傢伙，睡它一會，趁這魚正安靜而穩定的時候。"

他把釣索緊握在右手裏，然後拿大腿抵住了右手，把全身的重量壓在船頭的木板上。跟着他把勒在肩上的釣索移下一點，用左手撐住了釣索。

只要釣索給撐緊着，我的右手就能握住它，他想。如果我睡着時它鬆了，朝外溜去，我的左手會把我弄醒的。這對右手是很吃重的。但是它是吃慣了苦的。哪怕我能睡上二十分鐘或者半個鐘頭，也是好的。他把整個身子朝前夾住釣索，把全身的重量放在右手上，於是他入睡了。

他沒有夢見獅子，卻夢見了一大羣鼠海豚，伸展八到十英里長，而這時正是牠們交配的季節，牠們會高高地跳到半空中，然後掉回到牠們跳躍時在水裏形成的水渦裏。

接着他夢見在村子裏躺在自己的牀上，那時正在颳北風，他感到很冷，他的右臂麻木了，因為他的頭枕在它上面，而不是在枕頭上。

隨後他夢見那道長長的黃色海灘，看見第一頭獅子在傍晚時分來到海灘上，接着其他獅子也來了，於是他把下巴擱在船頭的木板上，船拋下了錨停泊在那裏，晚風吹向海面，他等着看有沒有更多的獅子來，感到很快樂。

月亮升起有好久了，可他只顧睡着，那魚平穩地向前拖着，船駛進雲彩的峽谷。

他的右拳突然朝他的臉撞去，釣索火辣辣地從他右手裏溜出，他驚醒過來了。他的左手失去了知覺，他就用右手拼命拉住了釣索，但它還是連續不停地朝外溜。他的左手終於抓住了釣索，他仰起身子把釣索朝後拉，這一來它火辣辣地勒着他的背脊和左手，這左手承受了全部的拉力，給勒得好痛。他回頭望望那些釣索卷，它們正在滑溜地放出釣索。就在這時，魚跳起來了，使海面大大地迸裂開來，然後沉重地掉下去。接着牠跳了一次又一次，船走得很快，然而釣索依舊飛也似地向外溜，老人把它拉緊到就快繃斷的程度，他一次次把它拉緊到就快繃斷的程度。他被拉得緊靠在船頭上，臉龐貼在那片切下的海豚肉上，他沒法動彈。

這正是我們等着發生的事情，他想。所以我們來對付牠吧。

讓牠為了拖走釣索付出代價吧，他想。讓牠為了這個付出代價吧。

他看不見魚的跳躍，只聽得見海面的迸裂聲，和魚掉下時沉重的水花飛濺聲。飛快地朝外溜的釣索把他的手勒得好痛，但是他一直知道這事遲早會發生，就設法讓釣索勒在有老繭的部位，不讓它滑到掌心或者勒在手指頭上。

如果那男孩在這裏，他會用水打濕這些釣索卷，他想。是啊。如果男孩在這裏。如果男孩在這裏。

釣索朝外溜着，溜着，溜着，不過這時越來越慢了，他正在讓魚每拖走一英寸都得付出代價。這時他從木船板上抬起頭來，不再貼在那片被他臉頰壓爛的魚肉上了。然後他跪着，然後慢慢站起身來。他正在放出釣索，然而越來越慢了。他把身子慢慢挪到可以用腳碰到那一卷卷他看不見的釣索的地方。釣索還有很多，現在這魚不得不在水裏拖着這許多摩擦力大的新釣索了。

是啊，他想。到這時牠已經跳了不止十二次，把沿着背脊的那些液囊裝滿了空氣，所以沒法沉到深水中，在那裏死去，使我沒法把牠撈上來。牠不久就會轉起圈子來，那時我一定想法對付牠。不知道牠怎麼會這麼突然驚跳起來的。難道飢餓使牠不顧死活了，還是在夜間被甚麼東西嚇着了？也許牠突然感到害怕了。不過牠是一條那樣沉着、健壯的魚，似乎是毫無畏懼而信心十足的。這可怪了。

"你最好自己也毫無畏懼而信心十足，老傢伙，"他說。"你又把牠拖住了，可是你沒法回收釣索。不過牠馬上就得打轉了。"

老人這時用他的左手和肩膀拽住了它，彎下身去，用右手舀水洗掉黏在臉上的壓爛的海豚肉。他怕這肉會使他噁心，弄得他嘔吐，喪失力氣。擦乾淨了臉，他把右手在船舷外的水裏洗洗，然後讓它泡在這鹽水裏，一面注視着日出前的第一線曙光。魚幾乎是朝正東方走的，他想。這表明牠疲乏了，正隨着潮流走。牠馬上就得打轉了。那時我們才真正開始工作啦。

等他覺得把右手在水裏泡的時間夠長了，他把它拿出水來，朝它瞧着。

"情況不壞，"他說。"疼痛對一條漢子來說，算不上甚麼。"

他小心地攥着釣索，使它不致嵌進新勒破的任何一道傷痕，把身子挪到小帆船的另一邊，這樣就能把左手伸進海裏。

"你這沒用的東西，總算做得還不壞，"他對他的左手說。"可是曾經有一會，我得不到你的幫助。"

為甚麼我不生下來就有兩隻好手呢？他想。也許是我自己的過錯，沒有好好訓練這隻手。可是天知道它曾有過夠多的學習機會。然而它今天夜裏做得還不錯，僅僅抽了一次筋。要是它再抽筋，就讓這釣索把它勒斷吧。

他想到這裏，明白自己的頭腦不怎麼清醒了，他想起該再吃一點海豚。可是我不能，他對自己說。情願頭昏目眩，也不能因噁心欲吐而喪失力氣。我還知道就是吃了，我的胃也承受不了，因為我的臉曾經壓在它上面。我要把它留下以防萬一，直到它腐敗為止。不過要想靠營養來增強力氣，如今已經太晚了。你真蠢，他對自己說。把另外那條飛魚吃了吧。

它就在那裏，已經洗乾淨，就可以吃了，他就用左手把它撿起，吃起來，細細咀嚼着魚骨，從頭到尾全都吃了。

它幾乎比甚麼魚都更富有營養，他想。至少能給我所需要的那種力氣。我如今已經做到了我能做到的一切，他想。讓這魚打起轉來，就來交鋒吧。

自從他出海以來，這是第三次出太陽，這時魚打起轉來了。

他根據釣索的斜度還看不出魚在打轉。這為時尚早。他僅僅感覺到釣索上的拉力微微減少了一些，就開始用右手輕輕朝裏拉。釣索像往常那樣繃緊了，可是拉到快繃斷的時候，卻漸漸可以回收了。他把釣索從肩膀和頭上卸下，動手平穩而和緩地回收釣索。他用雙手一搖一擺地拉着，盡量使出全身和雙腿的力氣來拉。他一搖一擺地拉着，兩條老邁的腿和肩膀跟着轉動。

"這圈子可真大，"他說。"牠可總算在打轉啦。"

跟着釣索沒法回收了，他緊緊拉住了，竟看見水珠在陽光裏從釣索上迸出來。隨後釣索開始往外溜了，老人跪下來，老大不願地讓牠又漸漸回進深暗的水中。

"牠正繞到圈子的對面去了，"他說。我一定要拼命拉緊，他想。拉緊了，牠兜的圈子就會一次比一次小。也許一個鐘頭內我就能見到牠。我現在一定要穩住牠，過後我一定要弄死牠。

但是這魚只顧慢慢地打着轉，兩小時後，老人渾身汗濕，疲乏得入骨了。不過這時圈子已經小得多了，而且根據釣索的斜度，他能看出魚一邊游一邊在不斷地上升。

一個鐘頭以來，老人一直看見眼前有些黑點子，汗水中的鹽份漚着他的眼睛，漚着眼睛上方和腦門上的傷口。他不怕那些黑點子。他這麼緊張地拉着釣索，出現黑點子是正常的現象。但是他已有兩次感到頭昏目眩，這叫他擔心。

"我不能讓自己垮下去，就這樣死在一條魚的手裏，"他說。"既然我已經叫牠這樣漂亮地過來了，求天主幫助我熬下去吧。我要唸一百遍《天主經》和一百遍《聖母經》。不過現在還不能唸。"

就算這些已經唸過了吧，他想。我過後會唸的。

就在這時，他覺得自己雙手攥住的釣索突然給撞擊、拉扯了一下。來勢很猛，有一種強勁的感覺，很是沉重。

牠正用牠的長嘴撞擊着鐵絲導線，他想。這是免不了的。牠不能不這樣做。然而這一來也許會使牠跳起來，可我情願牠現在繼續打轉。牠必須跳出水面來呼吸空氣。但是每跳一次，釣鈎劃出的傷口就會裂得大一些，牠就能把釣鈎甩掉。

"別跳，魚啊，"他說。"別跳啦。"

魚又撞擊了鐵絲導線好幾次，牠每次一甩頭，老人就放出一些釣索。

我必須讓牠老是痛在一處地方，他想。我的疼痛不要緊。我能控制。但是牠的疼痛能使牠發瘋。

過了片刻，魚不再撞擊鐵絲，又慢慢地打起轉來。老人這時正不停地收進釣索。可是他又感到頭暈了。他用左手舀了些海水，灑在腦袋上。然後他再灑了點，在脖頸上揉擦着。

"我沒抽筋，"他說。"牠馬上就會冒出水來，我熬得住。你非熬下去不可。連提也別再提了吧。"

他靠着船頭跪下，一時又把釣索挎在背上。我現在要趁牠朝外兜圈子的時候歇一下，等牠兜回來的時候再站起身來對付牠，他這樣下了決心。

他真巴不得在船頭上歇一下，讓魚自顧自兜一個圈子，並不回收一點釣索。但是等到釣索鬆動了一點，表明魚已經轉身在朝小船游回來了，老人就站起身來，開始那種左右轉動、交替拉曳的動作，原來他的釣索全是這樣收回來的。

我從沒這樣疲乏過，他想，而現在颳起貿易風來了。但是正好靠它來把這魚拖回去。我多需要這風啊。

"等牠下一趟朝外兜圈子的時候，我要歇一下，"他說。"我覺得好過多了。再兜兩三圈，我就能收服牠。

他的草帽被推到後腦勺上去了，他感到魚在轉身，隨着釣索一扯，便在船頭上一屁股坐下了。

你現在忙你的吧，魚啊，他想。你轉身時我再來收服你。

海浪大了不少。不過這是晴天吹的微風，他得靠它才能回去。

"我只消朝西南航行就成，"他說。"人在海上是決不會迷路的，何況這是個長長的島嶼[32]。"

魚兜到第三圈，他才第一次看見牠。

他起先看見的是一個黑乎乎的影子，牠需要那麼長的時間從船底下經過，他簡直不相信牠竟有這麼長。

"不能，"他說。"牠哪能這麼大啊。"

但是牠當真有這麼大，等這一圈兜到末了，牠在僅僅三十碼外冒出水來，老人看見牠的尾巴出了水。它比一把大鐮刀的刀刃更高，呈極淡的淺紫色，豎在深藍色的海面上。牠朝後傾斜着，魚在水面下游的時候，老人看得見牠龐大的身軀和周身的紫色條紋。牠的脊鰭朝下垂着，巨大的胸鰭大張着。

這次魚兜圈子回來時，老人看見牠的眼睛和繞着牠游的兩條灰色的鰦魚[33]。牠們有時候吸附在牠身上。有時候候地游開去。有時候會在牠的陰影裏自在地游着。牠們每條都有三英尺多長，游得快時全身猛烈地甩動着，像鰻魚一般。

老人這時在冒汗，但不光是因為曬了太陽，還有別的原因。魚每次沉着、平靜地拐回來時，他總能回收一段釣索，所以深信等魚再兜上兩個圈子，就能有機會把魚叉扎進魚身。

可是我必須把牠拉得極近，極近，極近，他想。我千萬不能扎牠的腦袋。我該扎進牠的心臟。

"要沉着，要有力，老頭，"他說。

又兜了一圈，魚的背脊露出來了，不過離小船還是太遠一點。再兜了一圈，還是太遠，但是牠露出水面，位置比較高些了，老人深信，再回收一些釣索，就能把牠拉到船邊來。

他早就把魚叉準備停當，那卷繫在叉上的細繩子給擱在一隻圓筐內，另一端緊繫在船頭的繫纜柱上。

這時魚正兜了一個圈子回來，既沉着又美麗，只有牠的大尾巴在動。老人竭盡全力把牠拉得近些。有那麼一會，魚的身子傾斜了一點。然後牠豎直了身子，又兜起圈子來。

"我把牠拉動了，"老人説。"我剛才把牠拉動了。"

他又感到頭暈，可是竭盡全力拽住了那條大魚。我把牠拉動了，他想。也許這一次我能把牠拉過來。拉呀，手啊，他想。站穩了，腿。為了我熬下去吧，頭啊。為了我熬下去吧。你從沒暈倒過。這一次我要把牠拉過來。

但是等他使出了渾身的力氣，趁魚離船邊還很遠時就動手，使出全力拉着，那魚卻靠攏了一點，便糾正了方向游開去。

"魚啊，"老人説。"魚啊，你反正是死定了。難道你非得把我也害死不可？"

這樣可甚麼事也辦不成啊，他想。他嘴裏乾得説不出話來，但他此刻不能伸手去拿水來喝。我這一次必須把牠拉到船邊來，他想。牠再多兜幾圈，我就不行了。不，你是行的，他對自己説。你永遠行的。

在兜下一圈時，他差一點把牠拉了過來。可是這魚又糾正了方向，慢慢地游走了。

你要把我害死啦，魚啊，老人想。不過你有權利這樣做。我從沒見過比你更龐大、更美麗、更沉着或更崇高的東西，老弟。來，把我害死吧。我不在乎誰害死誰。

你現在頭腦糊塗起來啦，他想。你必須保持頭腦清醒。保持頭腦清醒，要像個男子漢，懂得怎樣忍受痛苦。或者像一條魚那樣，他想。

"清醒過來吧，頭啊，"他用自己也簡直聽不見的聲音説。"清醒過來吧。"

魚又兜了兩圈，還是老樣子。

我弄不懂，老人想。每一次他都覺得自己快要垮了。我弄不懂。但我還要試一下。

他又試了一下，等他把魚拉得轉過來時，他感到自己要垮了。那魚糾正了方向，又慢慢地游開去，大尾巴在海面上搖擺着。

我還要試一下，老人對自己許願，儘管他的雙手這時已軟弱無力，眼睛只能間歇地看得清東西。

他又試了一下，又是同樣情形。原來如此，他想，還沒動手就感到要垮下來了；我還要再試一下。

他忍住了滿腔的痛楚，拿出剩餘的力氣和喪失已久的自傲，用來對付這魚的痛苦，於是牠來到他的身邊，在他身邊斯文地游着，牠的嘴幾乎碰着了小帆船的船殼，牠開始在船邊游過去，身子又長，又高，又寬，銀色底上有着紫色條紋，在水裏看來長得無窮無盡。

老人放下釣索，一腳踩住，把魚叉舉得盡可能地高，使出全身的力氣，加上剛才鼓起的力氣，把它朝下直扎進魚身的一邊，就在大胸鰭後面一點的地方，這胸鰭高高豎起，高達老人的胸膛。他感到那鐵叉扎了進去，就把身子倚在上面，把它扎得更深一點，再用全身的重量把它壓下。

於是那魚鬧騰起來，儘管死到臨頭了，牠仍從水中高高跳起，把牠那驚人的長度和寬度，牠的力量和美，全都暴露無遺。牠彷彿懸在空中，就在小帆船中老人的頭頂上空。然後，牠砰的一聲掉在水裏，浪花濺了老人一身，濺了一船。

老人感到頭暈，噁心，看不大清楚東西。然而他放鬆了魚叉上的繩子，讓它從他刮破了皮的雙手之間慢慢地溜出去，等他的眼睛能看清東西了，他看見那魚仰天躺着，銀色的肚皮朝上。魚叉的柄從魚的肩部打斜地戳出來，海水被牠心臟裏流出的鮮血染紅了。起先，這攤血黑黑的，如同這一英里多深的藍色海水中的一塊礁石。然後它像雲彩般地擴散開來。那魚是銀色的，一動不動地隨着波浪浮動着。

老人用他偶爾看得清的眼睛仔細望着。接着他把魚叉上的繩子在船頭的繫纜柱上繞了兩圈，然後把腦袋擱在雙手上。

"讓我的頭腦保持清醒吧，"他靠在船頭的木板上說。"我是個疲乏的老頭。可是我殺死了這條魚，它是我的兄弟，現在我得去做苦工啦。"

現在我得準備好套索和繩子，把它綁在船邊，他想。即使我這裏有兩個人，把船裝滿了水來把它拉上船，然後把水舀掉，這條小帆船也絕對容不下它。我得做好一切準備，然後把它拖過來，好好綁起，豎起桅桿，張起帆駛回港去。

他動手把魚拖到船邊，這樣可以用一根繩子穿進它的鰓，從嘴裏拉出來，把它的腦袋緊綁在船頭邊。我想看看它，他想，碰碰它，摸摸它。它是我的財產，他想。然而我想摸摸它倒不是為了這個。我以為剛才觸及過它的心臟，他想。那是在我第二次往裏推魚叉的柄的時候。現在得把它拖過來，牢牢綁住，用一根套索拴住它的尾巴，另一根拴住它的腰部，把它綁牢在這小帆船邊。

"動手做事吧，老頭，"他說。他喝了很少的一點水。"戰鬥既然結束了，就有好多苦工要做啦。"

他抬頭望望天空，然後望望船外的魚。他仔細望望太陽。晌午才過了沒多少時候，他想。而貿易風颳起來了。這些釣索現在都用不着了。回家以後，那男孩和我要把它們捻接起來。

"過來吧，魚啊，"他說。可是這魚並不靠攏過來。它反而躺在海面上翻滾着，老人只得把小帆船駛到它的身邊。

等他跟它併攏了，並把魚的頭靠在船頭邊，他簡直無法相信它竟這麼大。但他從繫纜柱上解下魚叉柄上的繩子，穿進魚鰓，從嘴裏拉出來，在它那劍似的長嘴上繞了一圈，然後穿過另一個魚鰓，在劍嘴上又繞上一圈，把這雙股繩子挽了個結，緊緊在船頭的繫纜柱上。然後他割下一截繩子，走到船梢去套住魚尾巴。魚已經從原來的紫銀兩色變成了純銀色，條紋和尾巴顯出同樣的淡紫色。這些條紋比一個人張開五指的手更寬，它的眼睛看上去冷漠得像潛望鏡中的反射鏡，又像宗教遊行隊伍中的聖徒塑像的眼睛。

"要殺死牠只用這個辦法，"老人說。他喝了水，覺得好過些了，知道自己不會垮，頭腦很清醒。看樣子它不止一千五百磅重，他想。也許還要重得多。如果去掉了頭尾和下腳，肉有三份之二的重量，照三角錢一磅計算，該是多少？

"我需要有支鉛筆來計算，"他說。"我的頭腦並不清醒到這個程度。不過我想那了不起的迪馬喬今天會替我感到驕傲。我沒有長骨刺。可是雙手和背脊實在痛得厲害。"不知道骨刺是甚麼玩意，他想。也許我們都長着骨刺，自己不知道。

他把魚緊緊在船頭、船梢和中央的座板上。它真大，簡直像在船邊綁上了另一條大得多的帆船。他割下一段釣索，把魚的下頜和它的長上顎紮在一起，使它的嘴不能張開，船就可以盡可能乾淨利落地行駛了。然後他豎起桅桿，安上那根當魚鈎用的棍子和下桁，張起帶補丁的帆，船開始移動，他半躺在船梢，向西南方駛去。

他不需要羅盤來告訴他西南方在哪裏。他只消憑貿易風吹在身上的感覺和帆的動向就能知道。我還是放一根繫着匙形假餌的細釣絲到水裏，釣些甚麼東西來吃吃，也可以潤潤嘴。可是他找不到匙形假餌，他的沙甸魚也都腐臭了。所以他趁船經過那片黃色的馬尾藻時，用魚鈎鈎上了一簇，把它抖抖，使裏面的小蝦掉在小帆船的船板上。小蝦有一打以上，牠們蹦跳，甩腳，像沙蚤一般。老人用大拇指和食指掐去牠們的頭，連殼帶尾巴嚼着吃下去。牠們很小，可是他知道牠們富有營養，而且味道也好。

老人瓶中還有兩口水，他吃了蝦以後，喝了半口。考慮到設置的障礙，這小帆船行駛得可算不錯，他便把舵柄挾在胳肢窩裏，掌着舵。他看得見那條魚，他只消看看自己的雙手，感覺到背脊靠在船梢上，就能知道這是確實發生的事情，不是一場夢。當初，眼看快要告吹，他一時感到非常難受，以為這也許是一場夢。等他後來看到魚躍出水面，在落下前一動不動地懸在半空中，他確信此中一定有甚麼莫大的奧秘，使他無法相信。當時他看不大清楚，儘管現在又像往常那樣看得很清楚了。

現在他知道這魚就在這裏，他的雙手和背脊都不是夢中的東西。這雙手很快就會痊癒的，他想。我讓它們把血都快流光了，但鹹水會把它們治好的。這真實的海灣中的深色的水是世上最佳的治療劑。我只消保持頭腦清醒就行。這兩隻手已經盡了自己的本份，而我們航行得很好。魚閉着嘴，尾巴直上直下地豎着，我們像親兄弟一樣航行着。接着他的頭腦有點不清楚了，他竟然想起，是它在帶我回家，還是我在帶它回家呢？如果我把它拖在船後，那就毫無疑問了。如果這魚丟盡了面子，給放在這小帆船上，那麼也不會有甚麼疑問。可是它和船是並排地拴在一起航行的，所以老人想，只要它高興，讓它把我帶回家去吧。我不過靠了詭計才比它強的，可它對我並無惡意。

魚和船航行得很好，老人把手浸在鹹水裏，努力保持頭腦清醒。積雲堆聚得很高，上空還有相當多的卷雲，因此老人看出這風將颳上整整一夜。老人時常對魚望望，好確定真有這麼回事。這時離第一條鯊魚來襲擊它的時候還有一個鐘頭。

這條鯊魚的出現不是偶然的。當那一大片暗紅的血朝一英里深的海裏下沉並擴散的時候，牠從水底深處上來了。牠躥上來得那麼快，全然不顧一切，竟然衝破了藍色的水面，來到了陽光裏。牠隨即掉回海裏，嗅到了血腥氣的蹤跡，就順着那小帆船和魚所走的路線游來。

有時候牠失去了這氣味的線索。但牠總會重新嗅到，或者只嗅到那麼一點，就飛快地使勁跟上。那是條很大的灰鯖鯊，生就一副好體格，能游得跟海裏最快的魚一般快，周身的一切都很美，除了牠的上下顎。牠的背部和劍魚的一般藍，肚子是銀色的，魚皮光滑而漂亮。牠長得和劍魚一般，除了那張正緊閉着的大嘴，牠現在就在水面下迅速地游着，高聳的脊鰭像刀子般地割破水面，一點也不抖動。在牠緊閉着的上下顎的雙唇裏面，八排牙齒全都長得朝裏傾斜。它們和大多數鯊魚的牙齒不同，不是一般的金字塔形的。它們像爪子般拳曲起來的人的手指。它們幾乎跟這老人的手指一般長，兩邊都有刀片般鋒利的切口。這種魚生就拿海裏所有的魚當食料，牠們游得那麼快，那麼壯健，武器齊備，以致所向無敵。牠聞到了這新鮮的血腥氣，此刻正加快了速度，藍色的脊鰭劃破了水面。

老人看見牠在游來，看出這是條毫無畏懼而堅決為所欲為的鯊魚。他準備好了魚叉，繫緊了繩子，一面注視着鯊魚向前游來。繩子短了，缺了他割下用來綁魚的那一截。

老人此刻頭腦清醒正常，充滿了決心，但並不抱着多少希望。光景太好了，不可能持久的，他想。他注視着鯊魚在逼近，抽空朝那條大魚望上一眼。這簡直等於是一場夢，他想。我沒法阻止牠來襲擊我，但是也許我能弄死牠。登多索鯊[34]，他想。叫你媽交上惡運吧。

鯊魚飛速逼近船梢，牠襲擊那魚的時候，老人看見牠張開了嘴，看見牠那雙奇異的眼睛，牠朝前咬住魚尾巴上面一點地方的魚肉，牙齒嘎吱嘎吱地響。鯊魚的頭露出在水面上，背部正在出水，老人聽見那條大魚的皮肉被撕裂的聲音，這時他用魚叉朝下，突然用力扎進了鯊魚的腦袋，正扎在牠兩眼之間的那條線和從鼻子筆直通到腦後的那條線的交叉點上。這兩條線並不存在。只有那沉重、尖銳的藍色腦袋，兩隻大眼睛和那嘎吱作響、伸向前去吞噬一切的兩顎。但那裏正是腦子的所在，老人直朝牠扎去。他使出全身的力氣，用糊着鮮血的雙手，把一支好魚叉向牠扎去。他扎牠，並不抱着希望，但是帶着決心和滿腔的惡意。

鯊魚翻了個身，老人看出牠眼睛裏已經沒有生氣了，跟着牠又翻了個身，自行纏上了兩道繩子。老人知道這鯊魚快死了，但牠還是不肯認輸。牠這時肚皮朝上，尾巴撲打着，兩顎嘎吱作響，像一條快艇般地劃破水面。海水被牠的尾巴拍打起一片白色浪花，牠四份之三的身體露出在水面上，這時繩子給綳緊了，抖了一下，啪地斷了。鯊魚在水面上靜靜地躺了片刻，老人緊盯着牠。然後牠慢慢地沉下去了。

　　“牠咬掉了大約四十磅肉，”老人説出聲來。牠把我的魚叉也帶走了，還有整條繩子，他想，而且現在我這條魚又在淌血，其他鯊魚也會來的。

　　他不忍心再朝這死魚看上一眼，因為牠已經被咬得殘缺不全了。魚受到襲擊的時候，他感到就像自己受到襲擊一樣。

　　可是我殺死了這條襲擊我的魚的鯊魚，他想。而牠是我見到過的最大的登多索鯊。天知道，我見過好些大的哪。

　　光景太好了，不可能持久的，他想。但願這是一場夢，我根本沒有釣上這條魚，正獨自躺在牀上鋪的舊報紙上。

　　“然而人不是為失敗而生的，”他説。“一個人可以被毀滅，但不能給打敗。”然而我很痛心，把這魚給殺了，他想。現在倒霉的時刻要來了，可我連魚叉也沒有。這條登多索鯊是殘忍、能幹、強壯而聰明的。但是我比牠更聰明。也許並不，他想。也許我僅僅是武器比牠強。

　　“別思索啦，老傢伙，”他説出聲來。“順着這航線行駛，事到臨頭再對付吧。”

　　但是我一定要思索，他想。因為我只剩下這件事可做了。這件事，還有棒球賽可想。不知道那了不起的迪馬喬可會喜歡我那樣擊中牠的腦子？這不是甚麼了不起的事情，他想。任何人都做得到。但是，你可以為我這雙受傷的手跟骨刺一樣是個很大的不利條件？我沒法知道。我的腳後跟從沒出過毛病，除了有一次在游水時踩着了一條海鰩魚，被牠扎了一下，小腿麻痺了，痛得真受不了。

"想點開心的事情吧，老傢伙，"他説。"每過一分鐘，你就離家近一步。丟了四十磅魚肉，你航行起來更輕快了。"

他很清楚，等他駛進了海流的中部，會發生甚麼事。可是現在一點辦法也沒有。

"不，有辦法，"他説出聲來。"我可以把刀子綁在一支槳的把子上。"

於是他胳肢窩裏挾着舵柄，一隻腳踩住了帆腳索，就這樣做了。

"行了，"他説。"我照舊是個老頭。不過我不是沒有武器的了。"

這時風颳得強勁些了，他順利地航行着。他只顧盯着魚的上半身，恢復了一點希望。

不抱希望才蠢哪，他想。再説，我認為這是一個罪過。別想罪過了，他想。麻煩已經夠多了，還想甚麼罪過。何況我根本不懂這個。

我根本不懂這個，也説不準我是不是相信這個。也許殺死這條魚是一個罪過。我看該是罪過，儘管我是為了養活自己並且給許多人吃用才這樣做的。不過話得説回來，甚麼事都是罪過啊。

別想罪過了。現在想它也實在太遲了，而且有些人是拿了錢來做這個的。讓他們去考慮吧。你天生是個漁夫，正如那魚天生就是一條魚一樣。聖伯多祿[35]是個漁夫，跟那了不起的迪馬喬的父親一樣。

但是他喜歡去想一切他給捲在裏頭的事，而且因為沒有書報可看，並且沒有收音機，他就想得很多，只顧想着罪過。你不光是為了養活自己、把魚賣了買食品才殺死牠的，他想。你殺死牠是為了自尊心，因為你是個漁夫。牠活着的時候你愛牠，牠死了你還是愛牠。如果你愛牠，殺死牠就不是罪過。難道，是更大的罪過嗎？

"你想得太多了，老傢伙，"他說出聲來。

但是你很樂意殺死那條登多索鯊，他想。牠跟你一樣，靠吃活魚維持生命。牠不是食腐動物，也不像有些鯊魚那樣，只知道游來游去滿足食慾。牠是美麗而崇高的，見甚麼都不怕。

"我殺死牠是為了自衛，"老人說出聲來。"而且殺得很乾淨利落。"

再說，他想，每樣東西都殺死別的東西，不過方式不同罷了。捕魚養活了我，同樣也快把我害死了。那男孩使我活得下去，他想。我不能過份地欺騙自己。

他把身子探出船舷，從魚身上被鯊魚咬過的地方撕下一塊肉。他咀嚼着，覺得肉質很好，味道鮮美。又堅實又多汁，像牲口的肉，不過不是紅色的。一點筋也沒有，他知道在市場上能賣最高的價錢。可是沒有辦法讓它的氣味不散佈到水裏去，老人知道糟糕透頂的時刻就快來到。

風持續地吹着。它稍微轉向東北方，他明白這表明它不會停息。老人朝前方望去，不見一絲帆影，也看不見任何一隻船的船身或冒出的煙。只有從他船頭下躍起的飛魚，向兩邊逃去，還有一攤攤黃色的馬尾藻。他連一隻鳥也看不見。

他已經航行了兩個鐘頭，在船梢歇着，有時候從大馬林魚身上撕下一點肉來嚼，努力休息，保持精力，這時他看到了兩條鯊魚中首先露面的那一條。

"Ay，"他說出聲來。這個詞是沒法翻譯的，也許不過是一個響聲，就像一個人覺得釘子穿過他的雙手、釘進木頭時不由自主地發出的聲音。

"加拉諾鯊[36]，"他說出聲來。他看見另一片鰭在第一片的背後冒出水來，根據這褐色的三角形鰭和甩來甩去的尾巴，認出牠們正是鏟鼻鯊。牠們嗅到了血腥味，激動起來，因為餓昏了頭，激動得一會迷失了臭跡，一會又嗅到了。可是牠們始終在逼近。

老人緊緊帆腳索，卡住了舵柄。然後他拿起上面綁着刀子的槳。他盡量輕巧地把它舉起來，因為他的雙手痛得不聽使喚了。隨後他把手張開，再輕輕捏住了槳，讓雙手鬆弛下來。他緊緊地把手合攏，讓它們忍受着痛楚而不致縮回去，一面注視着鯊魚在過來。他這時看得見牠們那又寬又扁的鏟子形的頭，和尖端呈白色的寬闊的胸鰭。牠們是惡毒的鯊魚，氣味難聞，既殺害其他的魚，也吃腐爛的死魚，飢餓的時候，牠們會咬船上的槳或者舵。就是這些鯊魚，會趁海龜在水面上睡覺的時候咬掉牠們的腳和鰭狀肢，如果碰到飢餓的時候，也會在水裏襲擊人，即使這人身上並沒有魚血或黏液的腥味。

"Ay，"老人説。"加拉諾鯊。來吧，加拉諾鯊。"

牠們來啦。但是牠們來的方式和那條灰鯖鯊的不同。有一條鯊魚轉了個身，鑽到小帆船底下不見了，等牠用嘴拉扯死魚時，老人覺得小船在晃動。另一條用牠一條縫似的黃眼睛注視着老人，然後飛快地游來，半圓形的上下顎大大地張開着，朝魚身上被咬過的地方咬去。牠褐色的頭頂以及腦子跟脊髓相連處的背脊上有道清清楚楚的紋路，老人把綁在槳上的刀子朝那交叉點扎進去，拔出來，再扎進這鯊魚的黃色貓眼。鯊魚放開了咬住的魚，身子朝下溜，臨死時還把咬下的肉吞了下去。

另一條鯊魚正在咬嚙那條魚，弄得小帆船還在搖晃，老人就放鬆了帆腳索，讓小船橫過來，使鯊魚從船底下暴露出來。他一看見鯊魚，就從船舷上探出身子，一槳朝牠戳去。他只戳在肉上，但鯊魚的皮緊繃着，刀子幾乎戳不進去。這一戳不僅震痛了他那雙手，也震痛了他的肩膀。但是鯊魚迅速地浮上來，露出了腦袋，老人趁牠的鼻子伸出水面挨上那條魚的時候，對準牠扁平的腦袋正中扎去。老人拔出刀刃，朝同一地方又扎了那鯊魚一下。牠依舊緊鎖着上下顎，咬住了魚不放，老人一刀戳進牠的左眼。鯊魚還是吊在那裏。

"還不夠嗎？"老人說着，把刀刃戳進牠的脊骨和腦子之間。這時扎起來很容易，他感到牠的軟骨折斷了。老人把槳倒過來，把槳片插進鯊魚的兩顎之間，想把牠的嘴撬開。他把槳片一轉，鯊魚鬆了嘴溜開了，他說，"走吧，加拉諾鯊，溜到一英里深的水裏去吧。去找你的朋友，也許那是你的媽媽吧。"

老人擦了擦刀刃，把槳放下。然後他摸到了帆腳索，帆鼓起來了，他把小帆船順着原來的航線駛去。

"牠們一定把這魚吃掉了四份之一，而且都是上好的肉，"他說出聲來。"但願這是一場夢，我根本沒有釣上它。我為這事感到真抱歉，魚啊。這把一切都搞糟啦。"他頓住了，此刻不想朝魚望了。它流盡了血，被海水沖刷着，看上去像鏡子背面鍍的銀色，身上的條紋依舊看得出來。

"我原不該出海這麼遠的，魚啊，"他說。"對你對我都不好。我感到抱歉，魚啊。"

行了，他對自己說。留意看看那綁刀子的繩子，看看有沒有斷。然後把你的手弄好，因為還有鯊魚要來。

"但願有塊石頭可以磨磨刀，"老人檢查了綁在槳把子上的刀子後說。"我原該帶一塊磨石來的。"你該帶來的東西可多哪，他想。但是你沒有帶來，老傢伙啊。現在可不是想你缺乏甚麼東西的時候，想想你用手頭現有的東西能做甚麼事吧。

"你給了我多少忠告啊，"他說出聲來。"我聽得厭死啦。"

他把舵柄夾在胳肢窩裏，把雙手都浸在水裏，小帆船朝前駛去。

"天知道最後那條鯊魚咬掉了多少魚肉，"他說。"這船現在可輕多了。"他不願去想那魚殘缺不全的肚子。他知道鯊魚每次突然撞上去，總要撕去一點肉，還知道魚此刻給所有的鯊魚留下了一道臭跡，寬得像一條公路，穿過海面。

這條魚可以供養一個人整整一個冬天，他想。別想這個啦。還是休息休息，把你的雙手養好，保護這剩下的魚肉吧。水裏的血腥氣這樣濃，我手上的血腥氣就算不上甚麼了。再說，這雙手出的血也不多。給割破的地方都算不上甚麼。出了血也許能使我的左手不再抽筋。

我現在還有甚麼事可想？他想。甚麼也沒有。我必須甚麼也不想，等待下一條鯊魚來。但願這真是一場夢，他想。不過誰說得準呢？也許結果會是圓滿的。

接着來的鯊魚是條單獨的鏟鼻鯊。看牠的來勢，就像一頭豬奔向飼料槽，如果說豬能有這麼大的嘴，你可以把腦袋伸進去的話。老人讓牠咬住了魚，然後把槳上綁着的刀子扎進牠的腦子。但是鯊魚朝後突然一扭，打了個滾，刀刃啪地一聲斷了。

老人坐定下來掌舵。他都不去看那條大鯊魚在水裏慢慢地下沉，牠開始是原來那麼大，然後漸漸小了，然後只剩一小點了。這種情景總叫老人看得入迷。可是這會他看也不看一眼。

"我現在還有那根魚鈎，"他說。"不過它沒甚麼用處。我還有兩把槳和那個舵把和那根短棍。"

牠們如今可把我打垮了，他想。我太老了，不能用棍子打死鯊魚了。但是只要我有槳和短棍和舵把，我就要試試。

他又把雙手浸在水裏泡着。下午漸漸過去，快近傍晚了，他除了海洋和天空，甚麼也看不見。空中的風比剛才大了，他希望不久就能看到陸地。

"你累了，老傢伙，"他說。"你骨子裏累壞了。"

直到快日落的時候，鯊魚才再來襲擊它。

老人看見兩片褐色的鰭正順着那魚必然在水裏留下的很寬的臭跡游來。牠們竟然不用到處來回搜索這臭跡。牠們並肩筆直地朝小帆船游來。

他卡住了舵把，繫緊帆腳索，伸手到船梢下去拿棍子。它原是個槳把，是從一支斷槳上鋸下的，大約兩英尺半長。因為它上面有個把手，他只能用一隻手有效地使用，於是便彎起了右手，好好攥住了它，同時望着鯊魚在過來。兩條都是加拉諾鯊。

我必須讓第一條好好咬住了才打牠的鼻尖，或者直朝牠頭頂正中打去，他想。

兩條鯊魚一齊緊逼過來，他一看到離他較近的那條張開嘴直咬進那魚的銀色腹部，就高高舉起棍子，重重地打下去，砰的一聲打在鯊魚寬闊的頭頂上。棍子落下去，他覺得好像打在堅韌的橡膠上。但也感覺到堅硬的骨頭，就趁鯊魚從那魚身上朝下溜的時候，再重重地朝牠鼻尖上打了一下。

另一條鯊魚剛才竄來後就走了，這時又張大了嘴撲上來。牠一頭撞在魚身上，閉上兩顎，老人看見一塊塊白色的魚肉從牠嘴角漏出來。他掄起棍子朝牠打去，只打中了頭部，鯊魚朝他看看，把咬在嘴裏的肉一口撕下。老人趁牠溜開去把肉嚥下時，又掄起棍子朝牠打下去，可只打中了那厚實堅韌的橡膠般的地方。

"來吧，加拉諾鯊，"老人說。"再過來吧。"

鯊魚衝上前來，老人趁牠合上兩顎時給了牠一下。他結結實實地打中了牠，是把棍子舉得盡量高才打下去的。這一次他感到打中了腦子後部的骨頭，於是朝同一部位又是一下，鯊魚呆滯地撕下嘴裏咬着的魚肉，從魚身邊溜下水去。

老人守望着，等牠再來，可是兩條鯊魚都沒有露面。接着他看見其中的一條在海面上繞着圈游着。他沒有看見另外一條的鰭。

我沒法指望打死牠們了，他想。我年輕力壯時能行。不過我已經把牠們都打得受了重傷，牠們中哪一條都不會覺得好過。要是能用雙手掄起一根棒球棒，我一定能把第一條打死。即使現在也能行，他想。

他不願朝那條魚看。他知道它的半個身子已經被咬掉了。他剛才跟鯊魚搏鬥的時候，太陽已經落下去了。

"馬上就要黑了，"他說。"那時候我將看見哈瓦那的燈火。如果我往東走得太遠了，我會看見一片新開闢的海灘上的燈光。"

我現在離陸地不會太遠，他想。我希望沒人為此大大地擔心。當然啦，只有那男孩會擔心。可是我相信他一定有信心。好多老漁夫也會擔心的。還有不少別的人，他想。我住在一個好鎮子裏啊。

他不能再跟這魚說話了，因為它給糟蹋得太厲害了。接着他頭腦裏想起了一件事。

"半條魚，"他說。"你原來是條完整的。很抱歉我出海太遠了。我把你我都毀了。不過我們殺死了不少鯊魚，你跟我一起，還打垮了好多條。你殺死過多少啊，好魚？你頭上長着那隻長嘴，可不是白長的啊。"

他喜歡想這條魚，想它要是在自由地游着，會怎樣去對付一條鯊魚。我應該砍下它這長嘴，拿來跟那些鯊魚鬥，他想。但是沒有斧頭，後來又弄丟了那把刀子。

但是，如果我把它砍下了，就能把它綁在槳把上，這該是多好的武器啊。這樣，我們就能一起跟牠們鬥啦。要是牠們夜裏來，你該怎麼辦？你又有甚麼辦法？

"跟牠們鬥，"他說。"我要跟牠們鬥到死。"

但是，在黑暗裏，天際沒有反光，也沒有燈火，只有風在颳着，那船帆在穩定地拉曳着，他感到說不定自己已經死了。他合上雙手，感覺到掌心貼在一起。這雙手沒有死，他只消把它們開合一下，就能感到生之痛楚。他把背脊靠在船梢上，知道自己沒有死。這是他的肩膀告訴他的。

我許過願，如果捕到了這條魚，要唸那麼許多遍祈禱文，他想。不過我現在太累了，沒法唸。我還是把蔴袋拿來披在肩上。

他躺在船梢掌着舵，注視着天空，等着出現反光。我還有半條魚，他想。也許我運氣好，能把這前半條帶回去。我總該多少有點運氣吧。不，他說。你出海太遠了，把好運給趕走啦。

"別犯傻了，"他說出聲來。"還是保持清醒，掌好舵。你也許還有很大的好運呢。"

"要是有甚麼地方賣好運，我倒想買一些，"他說。

我能拿甚麼來買呢？他問自己。能用一支弄丟了的魚叉、一把折斷的刀子和兩隻受了傷的手來買嗎？

"也許能，"他說。"你曾想拿在海上的八十四天來買它。人家也幾乎把它賣給了你。"

我不能胡思亂想，他想。好運這玩意，往往以許多不同的形式出現，誰認得準啊？可是不管甚麼形式的好運，我都要一點，要多少代價就給多少。但願我能看到燈火的反光，他想。我的願望太多了。但現在只有這一個願望。他竭力坐得舒服些，好好掌舵，因為感到疼痛，知道自己沒有死。

大約在夜間十點左右，他看見了城市的燈火映在天際的反光。起初只能依稀看出，就像月亮升起前天上的微光。然後能一步步地看清楚了，就在此刻正被越來越大的風颳得波濤洶湧的海洋的另一邊。他駛進這反光的圈子，於是他想，用不了多久就能觸及灣流的邊緣了。

這下可結束了，他想。但牠們也許還會再來襲擊我。不過，一個人在黑夜裏，沒有武器，怎麼能對付牠們呢？

他這時身子僵硬、疼痛，在夜晚的寒氣裏，他的傷口和身上所有用力過度的地方都在作痛。我希望不必再鬥了，他想。我真希望不必再鬥了。

但是快到午夜時分，他又搏鬥了，而這一次他明白搏鬥也是徒勞。牠們是成羣襲來的，朝那魚直撲，他只看見牠們的鰭在水面上劃出的一道道線，還有牠們身上的磷光。他朝牠們的頭打去，聽到上下顎啪地咬住的聲音，還有牠們在船底下咬住了魚使這小帆船搖晃的聲音。他看不清目標，只能感覺到，聽到，就不顧死活地揮棍打去，感到甚麼東西攫住了棍子，它就此丟了。

他把舵把從舵上突然用力扭下，用它又打又砍，雙手攥住了一次次朝下戳去。可是牠們此刻都在前面船頭邊，一條接一條地躥上來，成羣地一起來，咬下一塊塊魚肉，當牠們轉身再來時，這些魚肉在水面下發亮。

最後，有條鯊魚朝魚頭撲來，他知道這下子完了。他把舵把朝鯊魚的腦袋掄去，打在牠咬住厚實的魚頭的兩顎上，那裏的肉咬不下來。他掄了一次，兩次，又一次。他聽見舵把啪的斷了，就把斷下的把手向鯊魚扎去。他感到它扎了進去，知道它很尖利，就再把它扎進去。鯊魚鬆了嘴，一翻身就走了。這是來襲的這羣鯊魚中最末的一條。牠們再也沒有甚麼可吃的了。

老人這時簡直喘不過氣來，覺得嘴裏有股怪味道。這味道帶着銅腥氣，甜滋滋的，他一時害怕起來。但是這味道並不太濃。

他朝海裏啐了一口說，"把它吃了，加拉諾鯊。做個夢吧，夢見你殺了一個人。"

他明白他如今終於給打垮了，沒法補救了，就回到船梢，發現那舵把的鋸齒形的斷頭還可以安在舵的狹槽裏，讓他用來掌舵。他把蔴袋在肩頭圍好，使小帆船順着航線駛去。這時航行得很輕鬆，他甚麼念頭都沒有，甚麼感覺也沒有。他此刻超脫了這一切，只顧盡可能出色而明智地把小帆船駛回他家鄉的港口。夜裏有些鯊魚來咬這死魚的殘骸，就像人從飯桌上撿麵包屑吃一樣。老人不去理睬牠們，除了掌舵以外他甚麼都不理睬。他只留意到船舷邊沒有甚麼沉重的東西，小帆船這時駛起來多麼輕鬆，多麼出色。

船還是好好的，他想。它是完好的，沒受一點損傷，除了那個舵把。那是容易更換的。

他感覺到已經在灣流中行駛，看得見沿岸那些海濱住宅區的燈光了。他知道此刻到了甚麼地方，回家是不在話下了。

不管怎麼樣，風總是我們的朋友，他想。然後他加上一句：有時候是。還有那大海，海裏有我們的朋友，也有我們的敵人。還有牀，他想。牀是我的朋友。正是牀，他想。牀將是一樣了不起的東西。你給打垮了，倒感到舒坦了，他想。我從來不知道竟會這麼舒坦。那麼是甚麼把你打垮的，他想。

"甚麼也沒有，"他說出聲來。"只怪我出海太遠了。"

等他駛進小港，露台飯店的燈光全熄滅了，他知道人們都上牀了。海風一步步加強，此刻颳得很猛了。然而港灣裏靜悄悄的，他直駛到岩石下一小片卵石灘前。沒人來幫他的忙，他只好跨出船來，獨立把它盡量拖上岸灘，緊緊在一塊岩石上。

他拔下桅桿，把帆捲起，繫住。然後他扛起桅桿往岸上爬。這時他才明白自己疲乏到甚麼程度。他站住了一會，回頭一望，看見那魚的大尾巴在街燈的反光中直豎在小船的船梢後邊。他看清它赤露的脊骨像一條白線，看清那帶着突出的長嘴的黑糊糊的腦袋，而在這頭尾之間卻甚麼也沒有。

他再往上爬，到了頂上摔倒在地，躺了一會，桅桿還是橫在肩上。他設法爬起身來。可是太困難了，他就肩上扛着桅桿坐在那裏，望着大路。一隻貓從路對面走過，去做牠自己的事，老人注視着牠。然後他只顧望着大路。

最後，他放下桅桿，站起身來。他再舉起桅桿，扛在肩上，順着大路走去。他不得不坐下休息了五次，才走到他的窩棚。

進了窩棚，他把桅桿靠在牆上。他摸黑找到一隻水瓶，喝了一口水。然後他在牀上躺下了。他拉起毯子，蓋住兩肩，然後裹住了背部和雙腿，臉朝下躺在報紙上，兩臂伸得筆直，手掌向上。

早上，男孩朝門內張望時，他正熟睡着。風颳得正猛，那些漂網漁船不會出海了，男孩便睡了個懶覺，後來跟每天早上一樣，到老人的窩棚來。男孩看見老人在喘氣，跟着看見老人的那雙手，就哭起來了。他悄無聲息地走出來，去拿點咖啡，一路上邊走邊哭。

許多漁夫圍着那條小帆船，看着綁在船旁的東西，有一名漁夫捲起了褲腿站在水裏，用一根釣索在量那死魚的殘骸。

男孩並不走下岸去。他剛才去過了，有個漁夫正在替他看管這條小船。

"他怎麼啦？"一名漁夫大聲叫道。

"在睡覺，"男孩喊着說。他不在乎人家看見他在哭。"誰都別去打擾他。"

"它從鼻子到尾巴有十八英尺長，"那量魚的漁夫叫道。

"我信，"男孩說。

他走進露台飯店，去要一罐咖啡。

"要燙的，多加些牛奶和糖在裏頭。"

"還要甚麼？"

"不要了。過後我會弄清楚他想吃些甚麼。"

"多大的魚呀，"飯店老闆說。"從來沒有過這樣的魚。你昨天捕到的那兩條也蠻不錯。"

"我的魚，見鬼去，"男孩說，又哭起來了。

"你想喝點甚麼嗎？"老闆問。

"不要，"男孩說。"叫他們別去打擾聖地亞哥。我就回來。"

"跟他說我多麼難過。"

"謝謝，"男孩說。

男孩拿着那罐熱咖啡直走到老人的窩棚，在他身邊坐下，等他醒來。有一次眼看他快醒過來了。可是他又沉睡過去，男孩就跨過大路去借些木柴來熱咖啡。

老人終於醒了。

"別坐起來，"男孩說。"把這個喝了。"他倒了些咖啡在一隻玻璃杯裏。

老人把它接過去喝了。

"牠們把我打垮了，馬諾林，"他説。"牠們確實把我打垮了。"

"牠沒有把你打垮。那條魚可沒有。"

"對。真是這樣。那是後來的事。"

"佩德里科在看守小船和打魚的工具。你打算把那魚頭怎麼樣？"

"讓佩德里科把它剁碎了，放在捕魚柵裏使用吧。"

"那張長嘴呢？"

"你要就把它留下。"

"我要，"男孩説。"現在我們得來商量一下別的事情。"

"人家來找過我嗎？"

"當然啦。派出了海岸警衛隊和飛機。"

"海洋非常大，小帆船很小，不容易看見，"老人説。他感到真愉快，可以對一個人説話，不再只是自言自語，對着海説話了。"我很想念你，"他説。"你們捉到了甚麼？"

"頭一天一條。第二天一條，第三天兩條。"

"好極了。"

"現在我們又可以一起釣魚了。"

"不。我運氣不好。我再不會交好運了。"

"去它的好運，"男孩説。"我會帶來好運的。"

"你家裏人會怎麼説呢？"

"我不在乎。我昨天捉到了兩條。不過我們現在要一起釣魚，因為我還有好多東西要學。"

"我們得弄一支能扎死魚的好長矛，經常放在船上。你可以用一輛舊福特汽車上的一片鋼板做矛頭。我們可以拿到瓜納瓦科亞[37]去磨。該把它磨得很鋒利，不用淬火，不然會斷裂的。我的刀子斷掉了。"

"我再去弄把刀子來，把鋼板也磨好。這大風要颳多少天？"

"也許三天。也許還不止。"

"我要把甚麼都安排好，"男孩說。"你把你的手養好，老大爺。"

"我知道該怎樣保養的。夜裏，我吐出了一些奇怪的東西，感到胸腔裏有甚麼東西碎了。"

"把這個也養好，"男孩說。"躺下吧，老大爺，我去給你拿乾淨襯衫來。還帶點吃的來。"

"把我出海時的報紙隨便帶一份來，"老人說。

"你得趕快好起來，因為我還有好多東西要學，你可以把甚麼都教給我。你吃過多少苦？"

"多得很啊，"老人說。

"我去把吃的東西和報紙拿來，"男孩說。"好好休息，老大爺。我到藥房去給你的手弄點藥來。"

"別忘了跟佩德里科說那魚頭給他了。"

"不會。我記得。"

男孩出了門，順着那磨損的珊瑚石路走去，他又在哭了。

那天下午，露台飯店來了一羣旅客，有個女人朝下面的海水望去，看見在一些空啤酒罐和死梭子魚之間，有一條又粗又長的白色脊骨，一端有條巨大的尾巴，當東風在港外不斷地掀起大浪的時候，這尾巴隨着潮水起落、搖擺。

"那是甚麼？"她問一名侍者，指着那條大魚的長長的脊骨，它如今不過是垃圾了，只等潮水來把它帶走。

"Tiburon[38]，"侍者説。"Eshark[39]。"他想解釋這事情的經過。[40]

"我不知道鯊魚有這樣漂亮的、形狀這樣美觀的尾巴。"

"我也不知道，"她的男伴説。

在大路另一頭老人的窩棚裏，他又睡着了。他依舊臉朝下躺着，男孩坐在他身邊，守着他。老人正夢見獅子。

完

註解

1 查理斯・斯克里布納（1854—1930）為斯克里布納出版公司創辦人老查理斯（1821—1871）的次子，和其他兩兄弟一同繼承父親的產業，擔任主要負責人。麥克斯（韋爾）・柏金斯（1884—1947）為他手下的名編輯，從 1926 年初接受海明威的中篇小說《春潮》起，一直擔任他的責任編輯。本書出版時，兩人都已去世。

2 指墨西哥灣暖流，向東穿過美國佛羅里達州南端和古巴之間的佛羅里達海峽，沿着北美東海岸向東北流動。這股暖流溫度比兩旁的海水高 10 至 20 度，最寬處達 50 英里，呈深藍色，非常壯觀，為魚類羣集的地方。本書主人公為古巴首都哈瓦那東 7 英里的科希瑪海港的漁夫，經常駛進灣流捕魚。

3 就在科希瑪。

4 有些譯本將 dolphin 翻譯成鯕鰍。

5 位於中美洲尼加拉瓜的東部，是瀕墨西哥灣的低窪的海岸地帶，長滿了灌木林。為印第安人中的莫斯基托族居住的地方，故名。

6 王棕為加勒比海那一帶特產的特大棕櫚樹。在古巴被叫做 guano。

7 法國修女瑪格麗特・瑪麗・阿拉科克（1647—1690）於 17 世紀末倡議崇拜耶穌基督肉身的心臟，在信奉天主教的國家中傳播甚廣。

8 科夫萊為古巴東南部一小鎮，鎮南小山上有科夫萊聖母祠，每年 9 月 8 日為朝聖日。

9 這支紐約市的棒球隊是美國職業棒球界的強隊。

10 喬・迪馬喬（生於 1914 年）於 1936 年進洋基隊，以善於擊球得分著稱。1951 年棒球季後告別球壇。

11 這些是加勒比海地區老百姓的主食。

12 阿圖依為加勒比海地區印第安部族的酋長，被西班牙殖民者從海地島驅趕至古巴東部，於 1512 年被捕，給活活燒死。

13 美國職業棒球界按水平高低分大聯賽及小聯賽兩種組織，美國聯賽是兩大聯賽之一，洋基隊是其中的佼佼者。

14 指另一大聯賽，全國聯賽。這兩大聯賽每年各通過比賽選出一個勝隊，於十月上半月在雙方的場地輪流比賽，一決雌雄，名為"世界大賽"。

15 指費城的希貝公園，是該市棒球隊比賽的主要場地。狄克‧西斯勒於1948 年至 1951 年在該地打球。

16 該是指喬治‧哈羅德‧西斯勒（1893—1973），他於 1915 年開始參加大聯賽，於 1922 年第一次榮獲該年度的"美國聯賽中最寶貴的球員"的稱號。但本書故事發生在 30 年代，上文提及的他的兒子狄克不可能已去過露台飯店。這是個使評論家困惑的問題。

17 麥格勞（1873—1934）於 1890 年開始當職業棒球運動員，1902 年參加紐約巨人隊，兼任該隊經理，直至 1932 年，使該隊成為著名的強隊。他於 1906 年後就不再上場參加比賽。

18 J 為約瑟夫的首字母，在西班牙語中讀為"何塔"。

19 利奧‧杜洛奇（1906—1991）為三十年代著名棒球明星，1948 年起任紐約巨人隊經理，使之成為第一流的強隊。

20 阿道爾福‧盧克於 1890 年生於哈瓦那，1935 年前曾先後在波士頓、辛辛那提、布魯克林及紐約巨人隊當球員，後任經理。

21 四十年代後期曾兩度擔任聖路易紅人棒球隊經理。

22 舊時用來填塞船側的孔隙。

23 在北大西洋東部的一個火山羣島，位於摩洛哥西南，當時尚未獨立，隸屬西班牙。

24 測量水深的單位，每英尋等於 6 英尺。

25 西班牙語中的"海洋"（mar）可作陰性名詞，也可作陽性名詞，以前面用的定冠詞是陰性（la）還是陽性（el）來區別。

26 西班牙古地區名，包括今東北部四省。

27 貿易風，又稱信風，指的是在低空從亞熱帶高壓帶吹向赤道低壓帶的風。它之所以被稱為信風，是由於其出現規律如潮汐般有信，因此稱為「信風」；此外，古代商人用帆船進行航海貿易，靠的就是這種方向常年不變的風，故又名貿易風。

28 迪馬喬腳踵上的骨刺到 1947 年才通過手術割去，但後來有時仍有疼痛的感覺。

29 就在哈瓦那灣出海處的東端，和哈瓦那市區隔水相望。

30 位於哈瓦那東南，是古巴中南部瀕加勒比海的一個良港。

31 Rigel（在阿拉伯語中意為 "腳"）為獵戶座左下方的那顆最明亮的星，我國天文學稱之為參宿七。

32 指古巴這個東西向的大島。

33 鮣魚頭頂上有一個吸盤，常吸附在大魚身上，讓牠帶着游來游去。

34 原文為 Dentuso，西班牙語，意為 "牙齒鋒利的"，這是當地對灰鯖鯊的俗稱。

35 即耶穌剛開始傳道時，在加利利海邊所收的最早的四個門徒之一彼得。

36 原文為 Galano，西班牙語，意為 "豪俠、優雅"，在這裏又可解作 "雜色斑駁的"，是鏟鼻鯊的俗稱。

37 位於哈瓦那東的一小城，有礦泉，為避暑地，並有工廠。

38 西班牙語：鯊魚。

39 這是侍者用英語講 "鯊魚"（shark）時讀別的發音，前面照西班牙語習慣加上一個元音。

40 他想説這是被鯊魚殘殺的大馬林魚的殘骸，但説到這裏，對方就錯以為這是鯊魚的骨骼了。